Marcus Bourne Huish, Philippe Burty, Society Fine Art

Charles Méryon

Sailor, Engraver and Etcher

Marcus Bourne Huish, Philippe Burty, Society Fine Art

Charles Méryon
Sailor, Engraver and Etcher

ISBN/EAN: 9783337401214

Printed in Europe, USA, Canada, Australia, Japan

Cover: Foto ©Raphael Reischuk / pixelio.de

More available books at **www.hansebooks.com**

CHARLES MÉRYON,

SAILOR, ENGRAVER, AND ETCHER.

A MEMOIR

AND

Complete Descriptive Catalogue

OF

HIS WORKS.

TRANSLATED FROM THE FRENCH

OF

PHILIP BURTY

BY

MARCUS B. HUISH.

LONDON:

THE FINE ART SOCIETY, 148 New Bond Street.

1879.

NOTE BY THE TRANSLATOR.

IN prefenting to Englifh Collectors, in a revifed and acceffible form, the Catalogue which has hitherto been the ftandard authority on Méryon's works, I felt that my tafk did not end with the completion of the tranflation, but that a comparifon of the facts therein ftated with thofe difclofed by a careful review of the collections in this country was a neceffity. For affiftance in fo doing I muft tender my thanks to the authorities in the Print-room of the Britifh Mufeum, Mr. Seymour Haden, and the Rev. J. J. Heywood. The refult fuggefted confiderable alterations and variations, which Mr. Burty, after due confideration, affented to.

MARCUS B. HUISH.

AUX LECTEURS.

Le Travail fur *Charles Méryon et fon œuvre* que M. Marcus Huifh préfente aujourd'hui de ma part au public anglais était prêt depuis plufieurs années, et je n'efpérais plus rencontrer rien qui pût l'augmenter. J'avais eu dans la main tous les papiers défirables pour compofer la biographie, et j'avais noté tous les états des eaux-fortes. J'avais été follicité plufieurs fois de le publier.

Mais la France eft encore la proie de l'école académique. Les critiques et les amateurs qui combattent cette baftille imprenable font peu nombreux. Leur influence perfonnelle eft infuffifante pour réagir victorieufement, dans notre pays fi fortement centralifé, contre la protection accordée exclufivement aux doctrines académiques par les miniftères, les directeurs de mufées et de bibliothèques, les écrivains de revue, etc. Il en réfulte que les artiftes indépendants, étouffés dès leur entrée dans un monde univerfellement hoftile, végétant dans l'obfcurité, recevant mille railleries, font enterrés dans le filence. Tel a été le cas de Charles Méryon. Il a vécu miférablement. Il n'a jamais reçu un feul honneur officiel. Nos établiffements nationaux ont laiffé fortir de France les pages les plus belles et les plus rares de fon œuvre. La juftice commence feulement à fe faire.

Au commencement du mois de Juin dernier, M. Marcus Huiſh me demanda mon travail au nom des amateurs anglais. Je ne pouvais me refuſer à d'auſſi honorables et ſympathiques ſollicitations. Je ſavais d'ailleurs combien l'Angleterre ſ'était paſſionnée pour les œuvres de Charles Méryon. Il était temps que je miſſe en lumière tout ce qui pouvait ſervir à le faire definitivement connaître.

Dès 1859, je l'avais préſenté à la *Gazette des Beaux-Arts*, et je lui avais ſait commander des planches. A ce moment il était encore ſi peu connu en dehors du cercle des artiſtes et de quelques hommes de lettres, que mon premier article excita du mécontentement. On trouva que 'j'encourageais ouvertement l'abandon de la tradition.' Mais après le ſecond article, il y eut dans le bureau de la Revue une ſcène très-vive. Un des direĉteurs demandait avec ironie, 'Combien l'on accorderait de livraiſons à Raphaël, puiſque l'on en conſecrait deux à un aquafortiſte vivant ?' . . .

Je puis dire ſans manquer à la modeſtie, que mon heureuſe audace eut de bons réſultats. Les deux articles, l'un biographique et l'autre deſcriptif, furent conſtamment conſultés et cités par les amateurs d'eaux-fortes.

Je n'abandonnai jamais Méryon ni ſon œuvre. Lorſqu'il mourut je publiai de nouveau un article ſur les *Portraits*, lequel a reparu, revu et amplifié, dans mon livre *Maîtres et Petits-maîtres.** Enfin, lorſque je me décidai à me ſéparer de mes colleĉtions d'Eaux-fortes des

---

* M. Frédérick Wedmore dans ſon œuvre ſur Méryon, ſ'en eſt ſervi pour les anecdotes, de même que de mes autres articles et de mes converſations.

Maîtres modernes, les notes que je fournis pour rédiger le catalogue donnèrent fur fon œuvre des renfeignements abrégés mais certains.

Mes lecteurs comprendront fans peine combien je fuis heureux de voir fe répandre le renom d'un maîtrè que j'admire et d'un homme que j'ai aimé. Charles Méryon, avec Bracquemond, a été le principal reftaurateur de l'eau-forte artiftique en France. Sa gloire rayonne dans celle de ce vieux Paris qui devait fuccomber fous les conditions de la vie nouvelle, mais dont on regrettera toujours la couleur, l'originalité, la vérité. Il a ajouté un fleuron à la couronne de la nouvelle école françaife. Aujourd'hui, fes planches font difputées à prix d'or par les amateurs les plus difficiles. On m'a promis que fon nom ferait infcrit dans le nouvel Hôtel de Ville, parmi les noms dont fe glorifie la ville de Paris. Le peu que j'ai pu faire pour hâter l'éclofion de fa réputation eft une des meilleures fortunes de ma vie de critique. On comprendra que je tienne à honneur de rappeler les dates de mes premiers travaux fur Méryon, puifqu'ils ont fervi à tout ce qui a été écrit fur lui et fur fon œuvre.*

PH. BURTY.

19 *Octobre*, 1879, *Paris.*

---

* Mr. Wedmore dans fon catalogue n'a pas été trouvé une pièce inconnue, il n'a pas été fignalé un état important. On a feulement modifié—fans aucune raifon férieufe—l'ordre du claffement.

A MEMOIR.

HARLES MÉRYON, whofe work is now-a-days fought after with an avidity unexampled fave in the cafe of the rareft mafters, was born in Paris, the 23rd of November, 1821. He was of Englifh defcent through his father, Charles Lewys Méryon, phyfician and fecretary to Lady Stanhope, and probably compiler of the correfpondence of that cele-brated charaĉter. His mother, whom he always believed to be of Spanifh origin, although her name, Pierre Narciffe Chafpoux, is altogether French, was a ballet-dancer at the Opera. Intelligent and gentle, fhe beftowed on her fon the moft ardent affeĉtion, and watched over his early education with unceafing care. She, however, it was who bequeathed to him, together with an ardent temperament, the germs of the mental difeafe which carried him off whilft in mid career. She it was who made him the nervous child who fought for a reafon in everything. For inftance, one day he was taken to the Théâtre Comte. The lights were lowered, and a féance began. A fkeleton appeared, to be fhortly afterwards followed by a fecond. Both had fpades, with which they commenced to dig. Méryon was riveted by their occupation, but fuddenly became agitated, and afked to be taken home. When they got outfide the theatre his mother tried to

B.

pacify him, but he would repeat, ' Mamma, is it in order
to difguft men with agricultural purfuits that the Government fends fkeletons on to the ftage ?' When, forty
years afterwards, this was mentioned to him, he declared
that his nerves were ftill unftrung by the fcene.

At the age of five he was fent to fchool at Paffy.
From the firft he was an excitable and fitful fcholar.
He learnt but little Latin, devoting himfelf to the French
language. ' But,' he wrote, in fome notes which I have
before me, ' the charming fituation of the fchoolhoufe in
the open fields, the extent of the playgrounds, which gave
full fcope for races, athletics, and gymnaftics, and the
liberal diet of the houfe, all combined to develope my
health and ftrength.' He there received fome elementary
leffons in drawing from a mafter who had ftudied in the
ftudio of a landfcape-painter.

Thence he was removed to Marfeilles, and it was in
his long walks on the quays that he acquired a tafte for
a failor's life, which later on led him to enter the navy.
It was here, too, that he took his firft leffons in fwim-
ming, an art which he praĉtifed with confiderable fkill
and elegance, and which was conneĉted with the laft illu-
fions of his difeafed brain. From Marfeilles he travelled
to Hyères, where he delighted in the combination of
ruftic and maritime fcenery. Nice, Genoa, Pifa, and
Leghorn, were in turn vifited. He returned from Leghorn to Paris by way of Marfeilles. After paffing fome
time in a *penfion* he declared to his mother that he had
fixed on the fea as a profeffion, and with her confent,
after taking private leffons from Monf. Amyot, profeffor
of mathematics, he paffed into the Naval School.

It was at this time that he received a violent fhock,
which he told me afterwards caft over his life an in-
effaceable tinge of melancholy and timidity. He learnt
from the certificate which it was neceffary to produce

on admiffion that his name had not been legitimifed by his father until three years after his birth.

Méryon was in his feventeenth year when, in 1837, he entered the Naval School at Breft, under the number 47. He left it two years afterwards, with the number 12, and as a pupil of the fecond clafs. On the 15th of October, 1839, he failed from Toulon in the fhip *Algiers*, Commander Regandit, bound for Algiers, Tunis, and the fhores of the Levant. At Smyrna he was transferred from the *Algiers* to the 'three-decker,' the *Montebello*, with the grade of firft-clafs cadet. A few months fpent in cruifing about thefe coafts, fo full of memories of the claffic age, imparted a more healthy tone to his mind, and acted as a relaxation after the fatigue he had under-gone in the ftudy of mathematics. He was already bufy with his pencil, and he made various drawings, amongft them one of that gem of Greek architecture, the choragic monument of Lyficrates,* and another of the frieze of the Temple of Thefeus. He was alfo fortunate in vifiting Milo, Athens, Argos, the Tomb of Agamemnon, and the Gate of the Lions. The fact foon dawned on him that to make a good draughtfman education was neceffary, and fo, on his return to Toulon, he at once placed himfelf under the tuition of a profeffor of that city, M. Cordouan, a well-known painter of fouthern landfcapes. Rapid leffons in pencil, Indian ink, fepia, and water-colour drawing, fhowed him the various methods of execution, but natu-rally did but little to unfold to him the fecrets of the art. The works which he produced whilft under this tutelage are woolly in appearance, and lack knowledge of half tints, but the actual drawing is correct and deli-cate.

When Méryon, who had meantime loft his mother,

* He availed himfelf of this drawing to make his beautiful etching, *The Entrance of the Convent of the French Capucines at Athens.*

again went to fea at his own requeft, he was gazetted to the floop-of-war *Rhine*, Commander Bérard. On board fhip his paffion for art did not abate. He ftarted by painting the fcenes for an improvifed theatre; and whilft on the tour of circumnavigation, and during his ftay at Akaroa (in the Banks Peninfula), the forefts of New Zealand, the mountains of New Caledonia, the views of the coaft and iflands, the various types of favages, trees, vegetables, and animals, all furnifhed a thoufand fubjects for his pencil or his brufh. In the Catalogue will be found feveral etchings, which were intended by him to illuftrate a volume of travels of a fcientific nature.

I may here mention fome characteriftic traits of the man brought out during this voyage. ·

At Akaroa he tried his hand at fculpture. Monf. A. de Salicis, who was a brother-officer on board, has preferved the mould of a mafk of a ' grotefque favage, whofe large laughing face would, but for the formidable fet of teeth, pafs mufter for that of an antique faun ; and there can ftill be feen at the Jardin des Plantes, in one of the inner courts, a Model in plafter of a female whale (*Balæna auftralis*), caught in the Bay of Akaroa, Peninfula of Banks (New Zealand), reduced to an eighth of its natural fize, by M. Méryon, Lieutenant.' I have feen another example of his fkilful handicraft hung up in his ftudio in the Rue Duperré, a fmall frame in cork, in which he had placed a unique proof of the portrait of his friend Decourtives. He alfo, on the occafion of fome Chriftmas feftivities, carved a cradle in cork for the children in a family where he was received as a friend.

Later on in the Catalogue of his work the reflections which the fight of the deformity of man, and the mifery of his fellow-creatures in the large towns, aroufed in him, will be mentioned. The following letter of his about a dog, whofe portrait he has daintily engraved,

will fhow how his mind was always exercifed about every
thing and every body :—

'When we reached Sydney for the fecond time, we had a
New Holland puppy, of a favage breed, given us. He was of a
reddifh-drab colour, and appeared to be a crofs between a wolf
and a fox. It was interefting to watch his habits, not only whilft
croffing on our return voyage to Akaroa, but alfo during the laft
months of our fojourn at that port. He was far from being
fociably inclined, fhunning the failors, and loving the folitude of
the quarter-deck. We had at that time another dog, a little
bigger than our new-comer, a black one, called Noroi (a naval
abbreviation for North-Weft), for he came from the far North of
America. As regularly as the morning watch came round and
thefe dogs met, one paffing behind and the other coming down
from the poop, they fought. At firft the favage dog had the beft
of it, but afterwards the black one got the uppermoft. What,
however, was moft remarkable about this dog was his natural
inftinct, which appeared to be fharpened and developed in
him to a much greater degree than in the beft bred of our ordinary
fpecies; naturally enough, the principal aim of his life was to
fatisfy his appetites, which were not, I fhould fay, exceffive.
Anyhow, by combining this inftinct with a certain amount
of cunning, he accomplifhed certain thefts which one would hardly
have confidered poffible. At nightfall his hunting proclivities
feemed to awake; he fniffed the air, and went and came as if
anxious to be on the trail. The dog was intended for the Mufeum
at Paris, but, as ill-luck would have it, the day after our leaving
Akaroa for France, the fea having fuddenly got up, the dog, who
had not yet got his fea-legs, was precipitated by a violent roll of
the fhip into the fea, whence we dare not attempt to refcue him.
Being myfelf on the quarter-deck I was a witnefs to his fall.
Alas! all his inftinct and adroitnefs were futile to fave him. I
faw him cling with his claws to the projections on the fhip's fide,
and for fome feconds hang on above the abyfs below him; but I
had enough to do to hold on myfelf, as I had my hands full with
the fextant, with which I was taking obfervations, and fo I could
render him no fuccour. He loofed his hold, and fhortly afterwards
I faw him in the wake of the veffel, fighting defperately in the
breaking waves, with the albatroffes hovering round him, waiting
to make him their prey.'

Here is an epifode, too, of his feafaring life, which fhows in ftrong colours his aftonifhing tenacity of purpofe. It was told me by one of his fellow-officers.

The veffel was in the bay of Akaroa. Its captain, Bérard (who died an Admiral in 1872), acting under an exaggerated fenfe of difcipline, refufed to allow the officers to ufe his gig to go afhore in. The latter, on their fide, were vexed at having to ufe the ordinary failors' boat. Méryon announced that he would build himfelf a boat; fo, obtaining permiffion from the captain to go afhore for a time, he chofe out in the foreft, a fhort diftance from the fea, a yew-tree with a girth of more than four yards. He afked, but folely in order to economize the time, that this tree, which was very hard and of enormous fize, might be cut down by the fhip's carpenter. Once down, the frail and puny Méryon, compafs and pencil in hand, and armed with hatchet and faw, fet himfelf to work to cut out, fhape, and fafhion a boat five yards long. He flept under a fmall tent, and hardly fufficiently guarded himfelf againft the approach of wild animals by the fire which he kept up at night. He lived on provifions which his comrades, ftruck with admiration at his determination, brought him at intervals from the fhip. His hands, unufed to fuch work, were foon worn to the bone, but he rubbed them with a candle and bound them in bunting, juft as Bernard Paliffy relates he did during his years of refearch, and he worked on without ceafing. This lafted for three months!

When the boat was launched, its lines were fo well laid, and it exhibited fuch fea-going capabilities, that Captain Bérard was moved even to tears! And he gave orders that on their return to France it fhould be placed in the Arfenal at Toulon ; where, no doubt, it ftill exifts.

The cruife at an end, Méryon was given fix months' leave and returned to Paris. He had ferved with credit during the long and hard voyage. He, however, came to the conclufion that he was not endowed by nature with a conftitution fufficiently robuft to enable him confcientioufly to continue in a profeffion where fo much depended on health and ftrength. Although this feems to me, who have confulted his diary whilft on board fhip, to have been an ill-founded apprehenfion, he was fo impreffed with its reality that he confided his fcruples to his captain. This officer obtained from M. de Montebello, the Minifter of the .Marine, a promife that he fhould be attached to the Hydrographical Department. Unfortunately, this promife was not kept ; Méryon neglected to afk for an extenfion of leave. The revolution of February came unexpectedly. His pofition was a peculiar one. He was informed that he muft return to his old poft, but he replied that he wifhed to enter on another profeffion, and to give in his refignation as Lieutenant. He was owed five months' pay—he was in great ftraits, nay, almoft in want. Ultimately his refignation was accepted.

Thus it was that he left a profeffion in which all his old friends fay he would have done good fervice. On his leaving the fervice, on the 17th of September, 1846, he was in poffeffion of a fum of 20,000 francs, which his mother had left him. He eftablifhed himfelf in Paris, in the Rue Saint André des Arts, and, determined to complete what was wanting in his artiftic education, took a ftudio in the Rue Hautefeuille. He foon ftruck up an acquaintance with a painter employed at the War Office, by name Phelippes, formerly a pupil of David, and afked him to give him leffons. The ferioufnefs of this profeffor greatly impreffed him. Not only did he make him carefully copy in charcoal and with the pencil the plafter cafts of the Apollo Belvedere and the Olympian Jupiter, but, what was even of more importance, he explained to him their merits, and taught him to appreciate their beauties. It muſt not be forgotten that the ſubject of our memoir was now nearly thirty years of age, and at that time of life the hand is not ſo yielding or docile, nor does the mind derive from ſtudies which enforce ſubmiſſion that pleaſure which is afforded to younger minds. But to Méryon, whoſe genius was of an unquiet and independent character, this enforced obedience had for a certain time a ſalutary effect; and he was quite convinced that it would be uſeleſs for him to attempt to gain the object he had in view by a more ſpeedy route, by a leſs methodical education. But neverthelefs he had a hundred projects in his mind. He burned with a deſire to launch out into compoſitions of his own deviſing. After his ſtudies were only partially completed, he imparted to his maſter his longings to paſs to more advanced work. He made ſeveral anatomical drawings, in order to get more preciſe ideas on the play of the muſcles which cover the human frame. He went to the Louvre, inquired into the deep meanings of the maſters, of whoſe merits he was ſtill in-ſenſible, and for whom he never profeſſed a great reverence. I well remember his giving me a drawing in red chalk, which he had copied with minute exactneſs from the marvellous drawing from the hand of Raphael, repreſenting Pſyche holding in her hands a vaſe of cryſtal, and his ſaying, ‘In my copy I have been obliged to correct one of the eyes, which is not in its proper poſition.’ He alſo made at the Louvre ſtudies after the cartoons of Jules Romain.

But his deſire to meaſure his ſtrength—in fact, to run before he could well walk—overpowered him : ſo he ſtarted one fine morning, on a canvas ſix feet in length, the portrayal of an hiſtorical ſubject, ‘The Aſſaſſination of Marion Dufrène, captain of a fire-ſhip, at the Bay of the Iſles, New Zealand, the 13th of Auguſt, 1772.’ He took the account of the aſſaſſination from that publiſhed by

Crozat, the fecond in command to Dufrène, and he was aided by the fketches which he had made on the fpot of favages, trees, fruit, fifh, fifhing, and warlike implements. The preliminary drawing, which he fent to the Salon of 1848, has been preferved. It is at once original and forced. It is evident that it is the work of a hand furnifhed with precife and accurate knowledge of fubject, but wanting in power of manipulation. It is not worthy of a place befide his other works, his paftels, his minute fketches taken from nature for the purpofe of his etchings, nor the fine ftates of thofe etchings themfelves. Méryon next attempted to work out the compofition in oils. At the outfet he found himfelf face to face with difficulties. He was difcouraged, and left the canvas to effay another fubject, this time a purely allegorical one, infpired by the events of the revolution of February. Here again he was perforce compelled to halt midway, with the refult that he gave it up and entered the ftudio of M. E. Blery, the engraver.

It was foon found out that he fuffered from that affection in his fight known as Daltonifm, a difeafe much commoner than was fuppofed before fcience practically difcovered its effects. He could not diftinguifh the ripe fruit from the leaves in a cherry-tree or a currant-bufh. On his palette, in his box of paftels, he miftook red for yellow, pink for green; while certain colours, fuch for inftance as pure carmine, gold, cobalt, lapis lazuli, ftruck his fenfe of vifion moft powerfully and pleafingly. This notwithftanding he had a moft delicate faculty of diftinguifhing colours.

'One day,' fo one of his fellow-officers told me, 'we were fhooting fea-gulls from the quarter-deck.'

'"What colour do you make out their breafts to be?" afked Méryon.

'I replied, "A fpotlefs white."

"'You're wrong ; the colour's an inimitable rofe."
"'That's impoffible !" faid I ; "however, we'll foon
fee." And I covered the bird—fhot—the fea-gull fell on
the bridge, and I rufhed forward triumphantly to examine
its breaft. It was true ; its colour was in reality a falmon-
coloured rofe, of a tint certainly inimitable.'

Méryon was, however, not fo happy with his colours
in painting. I have a large paftel of his, a corvette
executing a difficult manœuvre. The veffel appears to
fkim over the top of the waves ; its fpreading fails liken
it to a huge bird flying before the ftorm. Méryon has
touched up the fpray which dances around and fhakes
againft the fides of the veffel with *red*, no doubt intending
to imitate the *bluey-green* of mid-ocean.* The error is
unmiftakable.

One Englifh and two French artifts impreffed him
more vividly than all the reft—'exciting all my fympathies.'
Thefe were Eugène Delacroix, Decamps, and Hogarth.
He had feen this latter's work during a fhort ftay he had
made in England, at the time when he decided to leave his
profeffor in painting, M. Phelippes.

He then alfo made a fhort excurfion into Normandy, to
Forges-les-Eaux, Eure. From thence he brought back a
few fketches of fcenery. He alfo went to Bourges.

'I there found,' fo he wrote, 'in the ftreets, on the
outfide of the houfes, moft curious effects of conftruction,
principally of a kind which is rapidly difappearing becaufe
it is not counted of fufficient importance to be either
reftored or preferved.' Of thefe he took fketches with
much avidity, and, in fact, returned two years afterwards
(1850-51) to finifh them on the fpot. Several of them
he etched.

---

* This picture, which comprifes the real and the fantaftic, has been
lithographed wondroufly well by M. Théophile Chauvel.

Whilft at M. Bléry's, Méryon confined himfelf to copying, fuch, for inftance, as a portrait of M. Bléry from a drawing of Eugène Buttura, a miniature of Chrift imitated from Philip of Champagne, copies of De Loutherbourg, Stephano della Bella, Salvator Rofa, Karel du Jardin. But the one who carried him away, and who made him an etcher, was René Zeeman. He found, and bought for a few fous, in the boxes which the fellers of engravings fet before their doors, and which have been of enormous fervice to young, indigent artifts, fome views of Paris and fome maritime fcenes publifhed in 1650. He was ftruck by the dexterous clearnefs of the lines made with the needle, with the quietnefs of the tone, and the brilliancy of the biting. He caught his ftyle, and, as a confequence, it characterifes the firft half of his work, which ends with the plate called the *Rue Pirouette aux Halles.*

Six months was the duration of his ftay with M. Bléry. Already his brain was flightly affected. He had fallen defperately in love with the daughter of the proprietor of a reftaurant where he took his meals, 'above all things on account of her charming voice.' But her parents would not hear of him. So, love-fick, he wandered through the ftreets of old Paris, of the old city fo teeming with intereft, fo grand in its buildings, with their maffive old windows framed in clinging leafage, and their lines broken up by turrets, and ftanding out with their pointed roofs againft the fky. From the window of his dark garret in the Rue Saint Etienne-du-Mont, which followed on to one another like the cabins in a veffel, he conceived the plan of that fet of etchings of Paris by which his fame is ever-laftingly affured, and the firft one on which he began was *Le Petit Pont.*

His plan of working was this. He feldom made a complete drawing on the fpot. He fixed on his fubject, and then he went patiently every day at the fame hour, and drew on fmall pieces of paper ftudies of the various portions, rigoroufly exact in their details. Thefe he either ftuck together when he returned home, or elfe made a drawing from them. The fergents-de-ville who made him move on, the curious ones who gathered round him, irritated him exceedingly, and made his work very unpleafant to himfelf. He ufed a very hard, fine-pointed pencil. He held this pencil as one holds a burin, and he worked with it in light and incifive ftrokes from the bottom upwards. He had been noticeable, when in the navy, for his finely-made yet ftrong hands. His keennefs of fight was remarkable. He could diftinguifh the fineft architectural details in a building as well as if he had ufed a telefcope. The affection of his fight before mentioned only impaired its capacity fo far as colours were concerned; it altered none of the other qualities of the fenfe, and confequently had no effect on that ftrong feeling of his which was either inherent or elfe ftrongly developed by obfervation and practice; namely, the relations which exift between light and fhade, between half tones and reflections.

Méryon, however, always had a tendency to exaggerate the fhadows. Were his firft plate, *Le Petit Pont*, taken by itfelf, one would be led to the conclufion that he had not yet learned to gauge the ftrength of the acid, and that he had in confequence over-bitten it. But the whole fet of Paris Views is imbued with a ftrength of tone which is not at all reprefentative of Paris, efpecially of that old Paris, which is always grey, and rather tender than fevere. His fineft work for quality of reflected light is the *Galerie Notre Dame*, the moft beautiful in effect of fky is the *Pont au Change*, whilft the *Abfide Notre Dame* is the moft remarkable for the harmony which reigns throughout. In that work he has fhown that, already a poet and a draughtfman, he was alfo a great colourift.

Méryon, in continuing his fet of Paris Views, bound

himfelf down to a principle never heretofore laid down, or likely in the future to be profeffed by any fchool, which proves that mafters in art will always be modifying its fet laws: he wrote in 1853 to a diftinguifhed artift, who had been one of the firft to recognife the originality and the value of his efforts,—'*La Pompe, Notre Dame,* may be taken as being a faithful reproduction of that building, which, it is faid, will foon be numbered with the paft. The towers of Notre Dame are flightly higher than in reality, but I confider this a permiffible licenfe, fince it is often in this way that the mind works when the object is no longer before our eyes, and the picture is compofed from memory.'

. He did not hefitate (and, as a confequence of his bold-nefs, his work is extraordinarily full of life) to take two fketches; one, for example, from the roadway, and the other from below, on the quay, to join them, and thus to treat the fpectator to a double view, and really afford him from the fame point of fight what he would in nature only fee in fucceffive ftages. See *Le Petit Pont* (38).

His firft proofs he ftruck off either himfelf or with the affiftance of that fkilled printer, Auguftus Delâtre, at his rooms in the Rue St. Etienne-du-Mont. He printed them on a green vergé paper, very thick, which added to their romantic afpect, with a biftre ink of excellent com-pofition; that is to fay, which filled the lines well, and did not flatten when the proof dried. He alfo ufed feveral quires of old vergé paper, whofe yellow tone feemed to impart funlight to the proofs ftruck off on it.

‘ The beft proofs,’ fo he wrote to me in 1863, ‘ thofe, in fact, which muft be confulted if an etching is to be properly judged of, are thofe printed regularly; that is to fay, when the plate is thoroughly wiped, the lines alone retaining the ink. The actual work is then fairly feen. Thofe, on the contrary, in which the ink by its diftribution over the plate co-operates in the effect, should be rejected, as lending a fictitious aid. When I first started I let myself oftentimes be led wrong through following what I know now to have been bad advice; but latterly I have come to the conclusion only to print in the usual or proper manner, which really required more skill on the part of the printer. There are, of course, cases where these proofs are really attractive, but they are exceptions which prove the rule. In any case it does not apply to my etchings, which are too simple and methodical in their manner of execution to require it.'

Méryon was not fond of imparting his methods of procedure. The following, however, are some details which artists will read with interest :—

'The varnish should be covered with ordinary black silk, of a double thickness and new. In varnishing the plate, the varnished side should be held downwards (however awkward it may be), so that the dust may not settle on it. When this varnish comes to be blackened, care must be taken not to put the flame too near the plate, or the varnish may be burnt. It is usually best before deciding on a varnish to be certain that it is in good condition, which it is if it remains greasy, or rather if it preserves the consistency of ordinary wax. The dabber ought also to be of double thickness, and the cotton which is enclosed in it new and free from dust. Beyond everything, care must be taken to remove grease or dirt from the plate; for that, nothing is better than whitening and water. There is a simple way of ascertaining the degree to which the plate should be heated—namely, to place upon it, whilst it is held over the flame of the spirit-lamp, the varnish and the dabber, when this latter will gradually lose its stiffness. Lastly, I said that it was necessary that the silk should be double for the ball of varnish, so it is for that; but for the dabber, if the silk is strong, it can be used of a single thickness. When the plate is smoked, it is necessary that it should be well heated, otherwise the varnish will burn, in which case it becomes brittle and loses its quality.'

Thus was the Paris set completed, not without innumerable obstacles, but yet with ever-increasing vigour and power. Included in it were the frontispiece, the verses which elucidated the hidden meanings of certain of the views, and the tailpieces. Méryon carried the set to the printseller, Vignères, and to Rochoux, and for the fifteen etchings, eleven large and four small, he asked the sum of thirty francs!

They met with no success, save with certain amateurs and artists of refined tastes, and with certain critics, such as Charles Baudelaire, Théophile Gautier, Paul Mantz, and M. Burger (then an exile). But in this small circle the success was a real one. The juries at the Salon could not see their merits. They refused, in 1853, the *Galerie de Notre Dame* and the *Rue des Toiles!* And though he exhibited on six occasions he never received a medal.

Of an extremely sensitive nature, endowed with a strong will, the pupil of no school, Méryon had taken the path pointed out by the school of romance, and which later on developed into naturalism. He translated, with that clear view which French genius always claims, the poetry, mysterious and grand, of that old Paris which it was reserved to the children of the second empire to see ruthlessly disfigured and destroyed. Under his needle, the architecture, which had hitherto been only rendered by the severe tracings of the architect, or by the summary in water-colours of the decorator, became what a landscape does under the pencil of the master of his art—namely, a Poem. He, as it were, borrowed of the reality only its features; he preserved the characteristic details of the construction and affixed to them the reflections of his melancholy or the secrets of his enthusiastic mind. Without sensibly modifying the appearance of the building, he invested it with both social and historical connections; as, for instance, in his etching of the building of the Morgue, which, without in reality altering, he drew in the likeness of a tomb. Thus his work has a twofold value. It takes its proper place in the portfolios of the collectors

of hiftorical documents.   It alfo properly adorns the walls
of the artift's ftudio.

In turning over his etchings, one is aftonifhed at the
mafs of matter which there really is in Paris for the poet
who ever contemplates it as a real and living being.   The
large fpaces of the quays, the river enlivened by the moving
veffels, the excited and tumultuous afpect of the ftreets,
the fhadows carried over the maffy walls, the windows
aligned and almoft touching, like the cells in a honey-
comb, the roofs and innumerable chimneys ftanding out
againft the fky,—what interefting matter for ftudy !   No
artift had ever before looked at Paris in this way, or had
thought of thus tranflating its innumerable graces.
Méryon, indeed, belonged rather to the middle epochs
than to our matter-of-fact and bufinefs-like age.   Therefore it was that he fo eafily reconftructed, in the midft of
the realities of the prefent, the probable appearances of the
paft.   On the earth we fee tall females talking to gigantic
workmen ; above, the flowers and creepers iffuing from
the balconies make frameworks to the windows ; above
that again the chimneys pour forth heavy wreaths of
fmoke, and higher ftill birds follow amidft the clouds the
quiet afcent of the balloon ' Speranza.'

Yet, again, he had the rare gift which has more than
once imparted youth to a fchool, namely, the gift of ornamental drawing, which without an effort can create what
are ufually called ' arabefques,' and which can only refult
from the alliance of a vivid imagination with an expert
hand.   The *Petite Pompe, Notre Dame,* and the *Addrefs of
Rochoux,* are beautiful examples of finenefs, clearnefs, and
fantafy.   They come like gleams of light in the clouded
fky of his brain.

Did a certain notoriety—we hardly dare to apply the
word ' fuccefs '—amongft the group of young artifts who
were bringing about a revival of the loft art of etching

bring any alleviation to his laborious exiftence? Alas!
no. He had fpent the money left him by his mother.
He had not even ever gained from the jury at the Salon
a medal which he could have taken to the pawnbroker.
The Imperial Print-room at the Louvre was actually in
ignorance of his exiftence. The dealer in etchings,
who now-a-days enriches the etcher known to fame,
and gives a livelihood even to the unknown, was not in
exiftence.

Méryon was almoft ftarving, when, whilft on his way
to depofit the regulation proofs at the office of the
Minifter of the Interior, he made the acquaintance of the
librarian, M. Jules Niel. This man, noted for his re-
finement and taftes, an eclectic amateur, who loved with
an equal love the French mafters of the fixteenth century
and the romantic works of Eugène Delacroix, grafped in a
moment the value of Méryon's work ; he interefted
himfelf in his life, obtained for him the purchafe of
feveral fets of his etchings by the Minifter, and orders for
copies to be made after hiftorical drawings : in one word,
he evinced for him the fincereft and moft ufeful intereft.
One may in truth fay that he prolonged his life. For
all this he was repaid only by the moft cruel infults; but
everything muft be condoned in an unconfcious being.

During the winter of 1855–56 the Duke of Aremberg
had feen at Montpelier the feries of Views of Paris. He
was fo impreffed thereby that he fent, in 1857, to Paris
for the artift, who was then worn out with work and
mifery, inftalled him in the village which adjoined his
château at Enghien, and afked him to reproduce, as and
when he liked, certain of the views in the park which he
thought the moft picturefque. He bought for him a
daguerreotype camera, and made him take leffons at
Bruffels in the management of what was then a novel
inftrument. But Méryon's mental difeafe foon fhowed

C

itfelf with extreme incoherence, and he returned to Paris in the month of March, 1858, hardly mafter of himfelf. He had taken a few photographs, the feleétion of which fhowed the fpecial tafte which he difplayed in everything. One fees the château (which, for the matter of that, has but little importance) beyond a park watered by a lake —a Pavilion built in a pure Italian ftyle—firft photographed entire, then only as to the portico—then a clump of trees :

' Thefe trees remind me of Leonardo da Vinci,' he faid, fpeaking of·an effeét of light. ' But after all,' he continued, ' however feduétive thefe ftudies may appear, in reality they are ufelefs. For how can you complete the whole when, as in this inftance, it is incomplete, fave as to a third, which if you change, all the reft falls to pieces ? Befides, the lines of perfpeétive are invariably falfe. In faét,' and on this he dwelt moft particularly, ' a photograph ought not to, nor ever can, enable an artift to difpenfe with a fketch. It can only aid him, whilft he works, by affurance and confirmation, by fuggefting to him the general charaéter of the aétuality which he has ftudied, and oftentimes by difcovering to him minor details which he had overlooked ; but it can never replace ftudies with the pencil.'

As an inftance of his ftate of mind at this time, I may here mention that one day M. Bracquemond went to fee him. He was out. His friends had taken the key to the porter. Méryon not returning, the vifitor took a pencil, and left as a vifiting-card a fketch on the wall—a fparrow with open beak darting down on a fly. Some days later, Augufte Delâtre, admiring this fketch, and feeing that Méryon did not reply, afked him if he had any complaint againft any one. ' If you care to know,' replied he, roughly, ' read on that wall my fate. I can no more avoid what is coming upon me than that fly can that bird.' His artiftic feeling did not pafs away, but he became daily more unfociable. *La Rue des Mauvais Garçons*, that mafterpiece of myfterious truth, like a mouth that makes one underſtand words without articulating them, is the elegant expreſſion of the ſtate of mind in which he then was. In the following month Méryon removed to the upper portion of the Faubourg St. Jacques, to a little ſummer-houſe which belonged to the mother of M. Léon Gaucherel, the painter and engraver. Here, throughout the day, he tilled every portion of a ſmall garden with feveriſh activity, not to plant and ſow, but in ſearch of imaginary bodies myſteriouſly buried there. His nights were terrible. This kind, inoffenſive, generous man, imagined his bed turned into a boat fighting againſt the tempeſt on an ocean whoſe waves were blood. But now and again he worked healthily. He drew in paſtels a corvette falling off from the wind, a large codfiſhing veſſel, and the ſhip *Le Vengeur* ſlowly and ſilently ſinking in the waves without a living creature on board, its colours nailed to the maſt, amidſt a gorgeous ſunſet whoſe rays form its apotheoſis.*

On his return from Belgium Méryon went to live in a miſerable little hotel in the Rue des Foſſé St. Jacques. There Delâtre would come and tend him. But this was no eaſy taſk. Méryon refuſed to leave his bed. He threatened with a piſtol thoſe who came near him.

On the 12th of May, 1858, the day after Flameng had taken his portrait (ſee p. 29), two officers of the law ſeized Méryon, who, without reſiſtance, allowed himſelf to be carried off to the aſylum at Charenton St. Maurice. He was then thirty-ſeven years old. In the certificate, taken twenty-four hours after admiſſion (a Government report, which is drawn up after the firſt examination of the patient), Dr. Calmel declared him to be ' ſuffering from melancholy madneſs, complicated by deluſions.' A fortnight after-

---

* Among the moſt beautiful drawings ever executed by Méryon is *Noon off Cape Horn.*

wards they reported a continuance of the madnefs. Little
by little, however, the difcipline of the afylum and good
living, following upon a life of ftarvation, produced a
beneficial effect upon the patient, and hopes were even en-
tertained of a cure. He gained the friendfhip of all thofe
who took care of him ; he was fo gentle and polite.
He fpent long hours in pufhing a wheelbarrow in the
garden. A ftudio had been given to him in order that he
might paint, engrave, and model. When M. E. Viollet-
le-Duc brought him his fketch, *The Ruins of Pierrefonds*
(fee No. 23 in the Catalogue), he found him in his little
cell occupied in making drawings in perfpective. Delâtre,
to whofe care were entrufted the coppers of the Paris feries,
ftruck off fome impreffions of them for the paper called
L'Artifte, and thus procured for him fome help. Thefe
impreffions were printed on imitation Chinefe paper, of a
wretched grain and a leaden hue, but they fhow the final
ftate of the plate, and for this reafon they deferve to be
collected. One can recognife them by the roofs being
generally left white, as if they had a ftrong light fhining
on them. Now-a-days, dealers who are not overfcrupu-
lous, feparate the Chinefe paper from the fmall-margined
mounts on which they were fixed, remount them on
vergé paper, imitating the plate mark, and felling them
for a great price as early ftates—as the *chefs-d'œuvre*, in
fact, which they formerly collected at five fous each from
the portfolios of the fecond-hand bookfellers on the quays.

On the 25th Auguft, 1859, Charles Méryon obtained
a holiday of three weeks, and was put into the hands of
M. Félix Foucou, with the permiffion of his old fhip
comrade, M. A. de Salicis, now captain of a frigate, and
Principal of the École Polytechnique. They were to take
him into Brittany. His releafe meant his ruin.

It was only towards 1856 that I knew him. I was
then ftudying drawing and painting with M. Chaffal-

Duffurgey, decorative painter attached to the Imperial manufactory of Gobelin tapeftry. I ufed on a Sunday to ftudy etching with an engraver, a very intelligent man, but with little talent, called Augufte Péguégnot. He had engraved fome picturefque but heavy views of Paris or its environs—*A Farm in the Rue du Cherche*—*Midi*—*the horrible abattoirs of Montfaucon.* He it was who firft fhowed me Méryon's etchings, near whom he had lived. The *Rue St. Etienne du Mont* aftonifhed, nay, almoft terrified me. For my profeffor was of the ftricteft fect of the Lyons fchool, who, following the teaching of their founder, Ingres, did not tolerate the leaft licenfe in colours, nay, even banifhed ' reflections ' from their work.

When I efcaped from him I went to learn by heart in the Print-room the works of Rembrandt, Claude Lorrain, the mafters of the fchool of Fontainebleau, and of a French mafter very unjuftly forgotten, Etienne Delaulne.

As regards Méryon's etchings, the feverity of the drawing foftered my youthful ardour, but the ftrength of his black and the ingenuity of his compofition appeared to me fimply heretical in their defiance of all rule. But when I left art for literature, and found myfelf amongft the colleagues whom M. Charles Blanc, formerly my mafter and my friend, had got together for the ftaff of the *Gazette des Beaux-Arts*, I thought of Méryon with the indulgence of a St. Anthony grown old, and fo caring little for the flefhly temptations which croffed his path. Méryon came one day to the office of the *Gazette des Beaux-Arts*, to offer a plate, *La Maifon du Muficien à Bourges.* But it was not like him ; his ftyle had loft its vigour, point, and force, and its myfterious influence over mind and eye. It was no longer of this Méryon that Victor Hugo could write to me as he did from the Guernfey rock :—

' Thefe etchings are magnificent things. We muft not allow this fplendid imagination to be worfted in the ftruggle in which it is engaged with the Infinite whilft ftudying Nature or Paris. Strengthen him by all the encouragements poffible. The breath of the univerfe breathes through all his works, and makes his etchings more than pictures—vifions.'

Even the copies that he made, fuch as *La Pafferelle*, or *La Vue du l'ancien Louvre*, had neither the exactnefs of the grand *Salle des Pas Perdus*, nor the effect of the *Pont Neuf et la Samaritaine*. The *Rue des Chantres*, which he did fo that he might perpetuate the beautiful fpire that M. Viollet-le-Duc had juft erected at the interfection of the roofs of Notre Dame, fhows fome of the beft of his old qualities. But the portraits which he executed for M. Benjamin Fillon (who fhowed great courtefy to him in all his tranfactions) coft him an infinity of trouble without proportionate refults. It was the fame thing with his *Souvenirs de Voyage*. They certainly fhow greater pains in their execution, more truth in the drawing of the places and in the epifodes which they contain, than is ufually to be met with in the engravings which are to be found in books of travel, but they were not fufficient to increafe his reputation as a great artift, nor even to fuftain it. The fcenes which he introduced into the *Rue du Collège Henri IV.*, and the *Miniftère de la Marine*, were the figns of an imagination no longer under control.

From this time, too, his method of working altered for the worfe. Timidity was apparent in his biting. He preferred to ftrengthen failing portions of his plates by work with the burin, which, if it has more brilliancy, certainly has lefs animation than effects produced by the acid. It is as regards this latter manner that Mr. Seymour Haden's opinion of Méryon is fpecially applicable ; Mr. Haden being one of the few who is competent, both as an artift and as a critic, to place himfelf alongfide of fo great a maſter.* In 1873 he wrote to me:—

'Certes Méryon eſt le "maître fur cuivre," le plus original et le plus artiſte que votre pays a produit. Je ne dit "eaufortiſte," car il n'a ni l'élan, ni la facilité manuelle, ni l'improviſation, ni cette faculté fingulière de la feleҫtion quant aux lignes eſſentielles qui diſtinguent l'eaufortiſte par excellence. Rêveur, réfléchiſſeur, piocheur, travailleur pénible, fe fervant conſtamment du burin, il eſt plutôt habile graveur qu'aquafortiſte furprenant, mais "artiſte graveur" bien entendu et de la plus haute diſtinҫtion.'

I had the pleaſure of being inſtrumental in getting him feveral commiſſions for plates from the *Gazette*, alfo from a few amateurs, and at laſt from the Imperial Print-room for the *View of the Ancient Louvre*. Mr. de Nieuwerkerke, the principal Direҫtor of Mufeums, behaved in this laſt matter with diſtinguiſhed courtefy.

Méryon at this time retouched the coppers of his Paris fet with the burin, thereby rendering them heavy and dull, ſtruck off fome thirty impreſſions from each, and deſtroyed them.

I went as often as I could do fo without indifcretion to pafs a ſhort time with him in his little *atelier*, No. 20 in the Rue Duperré. It was half filled with a wooden printing-prefs which the police allowed him to keep, and from which he ſtruck off his trial proofs. The walls were bare with the exception of a portrait of his friend Decourtive, in a frame which he had carved with a penknife out of a piece of cork, and which he had painted with water-colours; and a fern-leaf, to which he attached fome fort of fuperſtitious reverence.

I once furprifed him in the aҫt of waſhing the room with his feet bared, although it was winter. He was in a

---

* Mr. Hamerton has alfo fpoken well, and at length, of Méryon's genius; but his work, *Etching and Etchers*, is too well known to need quoting here.

good humour, and I fat down near him by the window.
He made me fit for the hands for two or three of the
portraits that he had been taking for the work *Poitou et
Vendée*. We talked at length, he of the undeferved ills of
his childhood ; of his mother, whom he adored ; of her
mother, who had had a difaftrous influence on her child,
having taken her to England after the events of 1815,
where fhe had cultivated her beauty more than her artiftic
faculties; of a fifter older than himfelf ; and finally of a
father who had made in England a rich marriage, and
had ever fince ceafed to think of him. I ufed to change
the converfation when he began to talk of his enemies and
of the fpies who followed him in the ftreets. His mind
quieted, his thoughts took a lengthy flight to the rocky
coafts of New Caledonia, where he faid he had met a
race of favages, handfome, heroic, intelligent, where
he had breathed an air ever laden with balm, where,
if he could, he fhould like one day to return to finifh life
free and happy, following the example of feveral of his
comrades. Then he was on the wing again, lofing himfelf in dark clouds. Somehow I always left him more
worried and difcouraged than I found him.

He never of his own free will touched the fubject of
art. He appreciated beyond everything the work of Bracquemond, but he knew hardly anything about art, though
he refponded to any queftion with a politenefs which, in a
lefs outfpoken nature, would have been taken for irony.
He had, however, an innate faculty of judging rightly.
One day he faid to me refpecting the portrait of Pierre
de Rivière, in which he had placed as an allegorical fur-
rounding a wheel crufhing the head and hand of a ftatue,—

' At certain dates every work of art that is not, without a
doubt, worthy of prefervation, fhould be deftroyed. Of the
fculpture, mortar fhould be made by means of an enormous
crufher. Of paintings they fhould make tarpaulins, fuch as the

failors cover packages with on board fhip. The artifts would be the firft to lend themfelves to fuch a fcheme, for if they had, for inftance, made a fecond-rate ftatue for the decoration of a monument, they would be enchanted to fee it replaced by a better. The whole world would be the gainers by it, from the models who pofe themfelves for the ftatues, or the cuftodians who watch over them in the Mufeums, to the hewer of the ftone and the draymen who tranfport it to the ftudio.'

'But,' I anfwered, 'have you ever reflected, my dear Méryon, as to who fhould compofe the jury to carry out your fchemes?' Whereat he laughed fo immoderately as to be heard in the ftreet; for on the rare occafions when he laughed it was the laughter of a child.

I had much trouble to obtain from him the biographical notes and the lift of his etchings, which I publifhed in the *Gazette des Beaux-Arts* in 1863. He made me promife only to mention as ftates thofe which he regarded as characteriftic. He afterwards annotated my work with minute care in a feries of letters, of which all but few, unfortunately, were incomprehenfible. A fhort time afterwards he quarrelled with me, without any real or apparent reafon, as he had with M. Neil. In his cafe he paffed an evening with him and his family. On the morrow, on their meeting on the quays of the river, Méryon advanced, refufed to fhake hands, and faid in the coldeft of tones, 'Vous êtes un voleur!' To me he wrote that I kept back in courfe of tranfmiffion the half of the fum which the Government had fent him for his work done for the Print-room; and he made the fame charge againft M. Rochoux, the printfeller, who had affifted him with an infinite tact and forbearance.*

---

* Mr. Haden, in his *Notes about Etching* (The Fine Art Society), mentions a fimilar inftance that occurred to him : 'One day, though I knew the difficulty of approaching him, I went to fee Méryon. I found him in a little room, high up on Montmartre, fcrupuloufly clean and orderly ; a bed in one corner, a printing-prefs in another, a fingle chair

But mifery followed hard at his heels. He took his meals at the meaneft of mean reftaurants, and he break-fafted for a few fous off fruit and fifh cooked in milk and flavoured with a few drops of vinegar.

It was impoffible to affift him, though his friends took the moft out-of-the-way means to accomplifh this end. Thofe who watched over him had again to call in medical advice, and Méryon was for the fecond time placed in confinement on the 12th of October, 1866.

The obligatory certificate, taken twenty-four hours after admiffion, reported 'typemanie chronique avec hallucination des principaux fens,' and the certificate at the end of the firft fortnight ftated that there were 'des fignes de délire partiel.' An obftinacy of will even to the point of death is the principal refult of this ftage of the difeafe. On certain days, however, he regained his fenfes,

and fmall table in another, and in the fourth an eafel with a plate pinned againft it, on which he was ftanding at work. He did not refent my vifit, but, with a courtefy quite natural, offered me, and apologifed for, the fingle chair, and at once began to difcufs the refources and charms of Etching. He was alfo good enough to allow me to take away with me a few impreffions of his work, for which, while his back was turned, I was no lefs fcrupulous to leave upon the table, what I was fure was more than the dealers would then give him for them ; and fo we parted, the beft of friends. But what followed fhows how, even then, his mind was un-hinged. I had walked fully two miles in the direction of Paris, and was entering a fhop in the Rue de Richelieu, when I became aware that Méryon, much agitated, was following me. He faid he muft have back the proofs I had bought of him ; that they were of a nature to com-promife him, and that from what he knew of " the Etched Work which I called my own," he was determined I fhould not take them to England with me ! I, of courfe, gave them to him, and he went his way ; and it was not till after his death that I became aware that he had, about the fame time, written to the Editor of the *Gazette des Beaux-Arts,* to caution him againft being taken in by me, and to impart to him the conviction that the plates which I pretended to have done were not done by me at all, but that, doubtlefs, I had difcovered and bought them, and figned and adopted them as my own !'

and on one of thefe his doctor took him to vifit the Exhibition of 1867, but a violent thunderftorm which occurred whilft they were there brought on at once a return of his exaltation. He could no longer work, though he wrote without ceffation long and incoherent memoirs. He allowed himfelf to die of exhauftion, believing himfelf to be Chrift held captive by the Pharifees, and being unwilling to wrong the feeble and outcaft by taking their food.

His lamp of life flickered out on the 14th of February, 1868, an hour after mid-day. Certain of his friends were informed of the fact, and gathered round his grave. I had previoufly feen him in his coffin. He reminded one of thofe mafks of wax which the French artifts of the middle ages moulded from the face before it was yet cold, then touched up and coloured and placed on the bier in the *chapelle ardente.* His fquare and projecting forehead feemed as if it had been protruded by the inceffant workings of the brain. His lips, large, thin, and clenched, fpoke volumes of that indefatigable and undauntable will which was fo evident in his work, either as defigner or engraver. His brown eyes were ftill wide open, and feemed to anxioufly and eagerly fcan the horizon for fome invifible object. So looks the failor when his veffel is finking, and he anxioufly wonders on what fort of a fhore the driving waves will fhortly hurl their fpoil.

Méryon had belonged to the Reformed faith. The hour, however, at which he was buried was the one at which fervice was performed, and fo none of the minifters could attend. M. A. de Salicis, his old comrade in arms, whofe name has often been mentioned in our fhort memoir, fpoke the following touching words :—

' Méryon is dead ! In this cold trench that eminent artift ends the firft part of his 'exiftence. In the flefh we fhall fee him no more ; but from to-day the Hiftory of Art will be incomplete without the name, for he was wanting in none of the qualifications requifite to fecure him a place in the illuftrious roll; neither in the talent, nor in, alas! that other effential—fuffering. Under the rule and the impulfion of the unfeen God, Méryon facrificed everything on His altar—youth's happy vifions, an enviable career, a patrimony, health, reafon. Above this poor troubled barque, at every inftant harried and urged onwards towards fhipwreck, there always hovered and fung a bird, whofe hue was of the pureft white. The barque has difappeared beneath the wave, but the fpotlefs bird, typical of his foul, has flown upward. Let us to-day forget to grieve for him who was called "Miferable Méryon," for he will henceforward be called " Méryon the celebrated " on earth, whilft the better part of him has already taken its place in the ferene atmofphere of eternity. What matters it now that he, like the reft of us poor human creatures, bore about with him imperfections, and if life was to him a time of fore trial? He has even now expiated that, and in the unknown world above there, he is enjoying that—the leaft of happineffes—which on earth he always ftrove for and never attained; for he now has—*Reft.*'

Charles Méryon refts in the cemetery of Charenton-Saint--Maurice, beneath a large flab of copper, on which his friend Bracquemond, his valiant comrade in art, engraved his titles and a mournful epitaph.

Paris, 1863–1879.

Three portraits enable us to form an idea of Méryon's perfonal appearance. The firft (dated 1852, by Bracquemond) refembles a medallion carved in ftone. The hair and the beard are long; the nofe retrouffé (this latter feature he is faid to have inherited from his mother); the features bony; the forehead ftraight and very lofty. The fecond portrait (alfo by Bracquemond) is a three-quarter length. Méryon, whofe coat is buttoned, is feated on a chair, the arm refting on its back. This picture was drawn from life directly on to the varnifhed plate. The features are more ftrongly marked in this fecond portrait than in the firft, which Méryon preferred. The eyes have a penetrating, reftlefs look, like that of a fawn who fees that it is watched. He was of middle height, nervous, and fupple, and I never knew him anything elfe but very thin.

The third and laft portrait, ufually known as ' Méryon Mad,' was taken by Flameng during the interval which elapfed between his return from Belgium and his firft confinement. Flameng, who could not fee too much of this ftrange, attractive face, came with a drawing-board, a fheet of grey paper, and fome black crayons, to the Rue Foffé Saint Jacques, and although Méryon did not lend himfelf to it, he drew a portrait full of character. Méryon in his fhirt, a large black cravat round his neck, is half fitting upon a little iron bed ; one of his knees raifes the counterpane and ferves to fupport the arm on which refts his head ; the other arm props up his body. The dark outline of his head, with its ftiff and ftubborn hair, is forcibly thrown on the wall by the flanting rays of the lamp. The face, with features fharp and emaciated by the fafting which he voluntarily impofed on himfelf, has the marks of fadnefs and irony.*

When this drawing was finifhed Méryon afked to fee it. He jumped out of bed and attempted to tear it to pieces. Flameng fled, upfetting his chair in his flight.

* The original of this drawing, which has been reproduced by means of lithography, is in the poffeffion of Mr. Seymour Haden.

Complete Descriptive Catalogue

OF

CHARLES MÉRYON'S WORKS.

N.B.—The titles and names printed in italics are Méryon's own, and are always found in fome one of the ftates, either in the margin or in the body of the impreffion. The titles printed in capitals and placed between inverted commas are names which we have affixed to the various plates in order to diftinguifh them.

The meafurements are in inches. They are made between the plate marks, or where thefe are not vifible, between the boundary lines of the work.

Irregularities of orthography or punctuation are always followed exactly, for they often, when fubfequently corrected, ferve as indications of different ftates.

The chronological order in which Méryon executed the work is followed in the four principal divifions :—

1. The Etchings made after Documents, &c. which comprife Nos. 1 to 26.

2. The Views of Paris which include Etchings, Nos. 27 to 53.

3. The Souvenirs de Voyages, comprifing Nos. 54 to 84.

4. Portraits, Nos. 85 to 97.

ERRATA AND ADDENDA.

P. 34. Note at bottom :—Mr. P. Horne (to whom I am indebted for many of the fuggeſtions contained in theſe Addenda) thinks the plate of *The Ewe* to be Méryon's, from the faꞩt that he has uſually ſeen it printed on the ſame ſheet as *The South-Sea Fiſhers* (14). The inſcription ſhould be '*0761. F V V A.*', *i.e.* Adrian Van der Velde fecit 1670, reverſed.

P. 35, line 6 from bottom, *for* Clément Jonghe *read* Clément *de* Jonghe.

P. 36. The firſt ſtates of *The South-Sea Fiſhers* and *Calais to Fluſhing* were before the angles of the coppers were rounded off.

P. 39, line 7 from bottom, *for* Gallery d'Apollon *read* Gallery of Apollo.

Mr. Horne remarks as to No. 19,—' I have a trial proof before any inſcription : a ſmall portion of the plate at the top, in the centre, is cleared as though intended for an inſcription. With the man ſitting on the parapet at the right is another man con-verſing—afterwards removed. The head of the man fiſhing in the foreground is not nearly finiſhed.'

P. 44, line 2 from bottom, *for* 4th *read* 3rd.

P. 45, line 3, *for* Polydes *read* Polycles.

,; line 7, *for* 21 *read* 31 ; inſert '*r*' between *imp.* and *des Feuillantines.*

P. 48, line 5 from bottom : the words *au Répu* ſhould be at the commence-ment of the inſcription.

P. 56. To the 3rd St. of *Le Petit Pont,* add, ' and with the bottom marginal line.'

In the 4th St. the ſpire on the right is ſlightly altered at the point where the work meets the roof of the houſe in front.

P. 57. Between the 2nd and 3rd States of *L'Arche du Pont Notre Dame* there are intermediate ones :—

1. With the Title, but before the addreſs of Delâtre and the *No. 3.*

2. The ſame as the 3rd State, but without the *No. 3.*

P. 60. Between the 4th and 5th States of *La Tour de l'Horloge* there are impreſſions having the inſcriptions of the 4th State and the gleams of light of the 5th.

P. 63, laſt line, *for* 110 *read* 4¼, and *for* 80 *read* 3⅛.

P. 64, line 10 from bottom, *eraſe* the words ' probably unique.'

P. 66, line 8 from bottom, *eraſe* the words ' before the final title.'

P. 70. *L'Abſide*, &c. There is a State between the 2nd and 3rd, in which the plate has been reworked and the date ' MDCCCLIV.' removed.

P. 74, line 11 from bottom, *for* Reuon *read* Pierron.

P. 92. *College Henri IV.* Mr. Horne has an impreſſion intermediate between thoſe in the 1ſt and 3rd States, with the buildings and mountains on the left, but no inſcription.

   ,,   line 7 from bottom, *add* the words, ' 4th State.'

P. 93, line 4 from bottom, *for* 4th St. *read* 5th St.
   The 4th State was alſo preceded by one which, inſtead of the Title, had merely Pierron's addreſs.

P. 94, line 3 from bottom. The verſe was alſo printed in red and in gold.

CATALOGUE.

D IVISION *No. I.*

Etchings made after Documents, Engrabings, Etchings, Drawings, Paintings, or Photographs.

---

1. ' LA SAINTE FACE.'

After a miniature made by Mdlle. Elife Bruyère, a pupil of Van Daël, from a painting of Philip of Champagne. This was the firft attempt at etching made by Méryon, under the direction of Monf. Bléry. We have never feen but one impreffion.

$h.$ 3⅛ in. $w.$ 2⅜ in.

2. ' THE COW AND THE ASS.'

A reverfed copy of an Etching of De Loutherbourg.

1ft St. Before ' *C. M. d'après de Loutherbourg,*' before working on the leg of the cow, and before the copper had been reduced in fize, as appears in the fecond ftate.

2nd St. With foregoing additions and alterations.

$h.$ 5⅓ in. $w.$ 3 in.

D

3. 'A Soldier.'

Standing full-face, and refting his two hands on a battle-axe. A copy of Salvator Rofa.   *h.* 5⅝ in. *w.* 3½ in.

4. 'A Shepherd.

A Shepherd carrying bundles follows fome goats, which defcend a hill. A fimilar copy after Stephano della Bella.
       w. 4¼ in. *h.* 3⅝ in.

5, 6, & 7.

'The Sheep and the Flies.'   *h.* 6¾ in. *w.* 5¼ in.

'The Three Pigs before a Hovel,' *and* 'The Two Horses.'   *h.* 6½ in. *w.* 5⅝ in.

Copies after three etchings of Karel du Jardin. Nos. 38, 8. and 4 in Bartfch's Catalogue.*

All three are figned ' *C. M. d'après K. D. J.*'

---

* The Britifh Mufeum claffes amongft its Méryons a plate of a Ewe and Two Lambs. In the body of the plate 'K di Jvva' below the number '4,' and ' Paris, imp. Delâtre.' *w.* 4 in. *h.* 3½ in.

·8, 9, 10, & 11.

'THE PAVILION OF MADEMOISELLE AND A PART OF THE
LOUVRE AT PARIS.'   *w.* 9⅝ in. *h.* 5¾ in.

'ENTRANCE OF THE FAUBOURG OF SAINT MARCEAUX AT
PARIS.'   *w.* 9¾ in. *h.* 5⅝ in.

'A WATER-MILL NEAR SAINT DENIS.'

'THE RIVER SEINE AND THE ANGLE DE MAIL AT PARIS.'

Tranſlations executed with much taſte, after a ſeries of
etchings by Zeeman (Nos. 55, 57, and 61 in Bartſch's Catalogue), originally publiſhed at Amſterdam, about 1650, by Clément
Jonghe, under the title of *Veues de Paris et ſes Environs.*

All four bear the inſcription, '*C. M.*' *or* '*C. Méryon d'après
Zeeman,*' and are the ſame ſize as the originals.

The coppers of the two firſt were bought of Méryon by the·
engraver, Auguſte Péquégnot, and are ſtill in exiſtence.

12, 13, 14, & 15.

'THE GALLIOT OF JEAN DE VYL AT ROTTERDAM.'

1ft St.   Before the little houfe on the bank, and before the
initials ' C. M.'

2nd St.   With the initials, but before the angles of the copper-
plate were rounded off.   The earlier ftates of this and the reft of
the fet were printed on India paper and mounted.

'FROM HAARLEM TO AMSTERDAM.'

1ft St.   Before the angles of the copper-plate were rounded off.

'SOUTH-SEA FISHERS.'

1ft St.   With the initials ' C. M.' at the left corner.

The magazine ' L'Artifte' publifhed a new iffue of this plate
in 1861, with the name of ' Méryon ' completed by a ftrange
hand.

'CALAIS TO FLUSHING.'

The four preceding plates were copies in reverfe of etchings
by Regnier Zeeman (catalogued in Bartfch under Nos. 7, 8, 13,
and 14), the fet having for title 'Recueil de plufieurs navires et
payfages faits d'après le naturel.'   w. 4¾ in. h. 2⅜ in.

16. *Entrée du Couvent des Capucins français à Athènes.*

Trial proof, in pure etching.

1ft St. Dry point work in the ſky to the right of the Plate, and before any letters. Some rare proofs of this ſtate are printed on large paper.

2nd St. With the title, ' *tome i. p.* 76,' in the upper left angle, '*C. Méryon Sculp.*' and the printer's addreſs, '*Pierron Delâtre, R. Montfaucon,* 1.'

This plate was reduced by Méryon by means of the 'chambre noire.' He availed himſelf alſo of a photograph from an engraving (No. xiii.) in a work entitled ' *Les Ruines des plus beaux monumens de la Grèce,* par M. le Roy, Architecte, MDCCLVIII.' Méryon's etching was made for a book of the Count L. de Laborde, '*Athènes, aux* XV. XVI. *et* XVII. *ſiècles, d'après des documens inédits. Paris,* 1854.'

The Capucines bought, in 1669, in the ancient ſtreet of Tripodes, this choragic monument of Lyſicrates.

In 1845 this lovely piece of ancient architecture was ſtill built up in a wall ; but it has ſince been detached, and now ſtands by itſelf.   *b.* 7½. in. *w.* 4⅞ in.

17. 'The Salle des Pas Perdus.'

In the lower margin are the words :—

'*Il faut avoir examiné la pièce originale dans ses moindres détails (comme j'ai été forcé de le faire) pour en savoir toute la beauté. Il va sans dire que l'architecture y est traitée de main de maître. Les statues des rois sont d'un grand style, toutes bizarres qu'elles puissent paraître au premier abord. Quant aux petites figures qui animent la salle d'une façon si piquantes, et qu'on pourrait également croire faites avec négligence, elles sont, je pense, des plus remarquables consanguinées, d'une certaine manière, avec celles de Reinier Zeeman, le graveur de navires, en ce qui concerne la vérité de la mimique, elles rappellent dans de certaines parties (les petites jambes surtout) la belle correction de Marc Antoine. Il n'est pas jusqu'à l'expression des masques, qui, quoique indiquée avec une naïveté presqu'enfantine, ne soit d'une grande science physiognomonique.— C. Méryon, sculp. d'après la pièce originale de Ducerceau, due à l'obligeance de Monsieur Destailleur, Architecte, Paris,* MDCCCLV.'

1st St. Before the above infcription, and with the margin of the plate *w.* 17⅓ in. *h.* 11⅘.

2nd St. With the infcription and the plate reduced to the dimenfions *w.* 16⅞ in. *h.* 10¾.

3rd St. With ' *C. Méryon sculp. d'après Ducerceau,* MDCCCLV., and *Delâtre R. Fg. St. Jacques, No.* 81.' The copper has been cut at the bottom, juft below the marginal line.

18. *Chenonceau.   C. Méryon fculp. d'après Ducerceau —
Delâtre, rue du faub. St. Jacques,* 81.

This very intelligent reduction of one of the plates in the
fecond volume of ' Les plus excellents baftimens de France, par
Jacques Androuet du Cerceau, Architecte à Paris,' is to be found
in ' l'Inventaire des meubles, bijoux et livres eftans à Chenonceau,
fuivi d'une notice fur le Château de Chenonceau,' by the Prince
Augufte Galitzin, 1856.   *w.* 7¼ in. *h.* 4½ in.

19. *Le Pont-Neuf et la Samaritaine au deffous la 1ère Arche
du Pont-au-Change.   C. Méryon fculp. d'après un
deffin de Nicolle, tiré du cabinet de Monfieur Deftail-
leurs, Architecte.   Imp. A. Delâtre, Rue Fg. . St.
Jacques,* 81.

Between the houfes which line the quai de la Ferraille (now
the quai de la Mégifferie), and the monument of the Samaritaine,
is feen the angle of the Gallery d'Apollon, with the Pavilion of
Charles the Ninth.

1ft St.   With a delicate fky.
2nd St.   Before any lettering, the bottom marginal line has
been ftrengthened and completed.
3rd St.   With the above infcription, and the publication line.
                                           w. 8 in. *h.* 5⅝ in.

20. *Le Pont-au-Change vers* 1784.   *C. Méryon fculp.*,
MDCCCL., *d'après un deffin de Nicolle tiré du Cabinet
de M. Deftailleur, Architecte. Imp. A. Delâtre, faub.
St. Jacques, No.* 81.

To the left above the roofs of the houfes is feen the top of
the Tower Saint Jacques de la Boucherie.
Trial Proof. Before the fky.
1ft St. Before the rope ftretched acrofs the Seine for the ufe
of the ferry-boat. The marks left by the vice when the artift
varnifhed his plate, have been erafed.
2nd St. With the rope, but before any lettering.
3rd St. With the rope, the title, and the publication line.

w. 9⅜ in. *h.* 5¼ in.

21. *Plan du combat de Sinope, d'après le deffin d'une officier du
navire anglais " Retribution."   C. Méryon fculp.
A. Delâtre, Imp. Rue de la Bucherie, No.* 6.

This plan, which fhows the refpective pofitions of the Ruffian
and Turkifh fleets, was intended to illuftrate a work which was
never publifhed.
Almoft all the impreffions have been coloured in water-
colours. They were fold in Paris by Charles Tanera.

w. 10¼ in. *h.* 7¼ in.

22. *San Francifco.* *C. Méryon del. fculp. Paris,* 1856.
A. Delâtre imp. Rue fᵉ· Poiffonnière, 145.

The foreground confifts of fields and wafte land. Beyond the city is depi&ed, but few important buildings are vifible. The harbour is full of fhipping.

This view of San Francifco in 1855 has become a moft interefting hiftorical document. The commiffion for the plate was given to Méryon by two bankers, Meffrs. Bayerque and Pioche, whofe portraits fill two medallions and whofe initials are placed on efcutcheons.

The arched frame, fupported by the figure of 'Work' feated on mining tools, and 'Abundance' reclining on fruits of various kinds, was not placed there for allegorical or ornamental purpofes merely, but principally in order to fill up a large gap which occurred in the five little daguerreotype plates which had been furnifhed to Méryon as a bafis for his defign. Thefe plates having been taken on the fpot, but at different hours of the day, fhowed in fome the light coming from the right, in others from the left. This troubled him greatly, as did the whole plate, which, in fa&, haftened on the courfe of his malady. He wrote to M. Burty :—

'Comme il arrive néceffairement par fuite de la nature même de l'inftrument, ces differentes vues ne pouvaient fe raccorder que d'une manière très imparfaite, la confufion et la non-verticalité des bords rendant la coïncidence impoffible. De plus, l'opérateur, pour obtenir l'enfemble, avait été forcé de faire décrire un angle très fenfible à la lunette, d'où réfultait une déviation confidérable des grandes lignes de perfpe&ive ; fi bien que, dans le centre furtout, il devenait obligatoire de remédier à cet accident capital. Autre fait inhérent à l'épreuve daguerrienne, les parties profondes étaient de plus en plus diffufes à mefure qu'elles f'éloignaient du point de vue de l'obje&if. Force me fut donc, avant de faire mon calque, de redreffer chacun de ces deffins.

'Se rendre compte,' continued he, 'de l'averfion que j'éprouvais à mener à fin cette befogne longue, ardue, ingrate,* eft chofe facile fi l'on veut fe mettre à un place. Il y avait de quoi rebuter l'homme le plus patient du monde. Ce qu'il y avait de dur pardeffus tout, c'était l'obligation de fixer attentivement ces objets, tantôt reproduits avec une précifion étourdiffante, tantôt au contraire diffus, quelquefois même

---

* He was to be paid 1200 francs for the Plate.

ayant fubi de telles déformations de lignes et de couleurs, qu'il devenait prefque impoffible d'en connaître la forme. C'eft ainfi que je ne parvins à démêler une efpèce de chapelle, à-peu-près, au premier plan, à droite, qu'après l'avoir cherchée, le daguerréotype devant mes yeux, dans mes moments de répit, pendant une huitaine de jours au moins. Il y avait, au centre furtout, comme un cahos, une fondrière, caufés par cette déviation des lignes dont j'ai parlé, qui me donnait le vertige. Le mal de cœur me faififfait inftantanément. Je me fentais tomber à la renverfe.

'Le jour où je verfai fur une planche couverte la traitreffe liqueur, par quelles émotions ne paffai-je pas ! Ce fut prefque pour moi une queftion de vie ou de mort ! Enfin, grâce à un Deftin propice, extraordinaire, il faut en convenir, le réfultat parut dépaffer mon attente. . . . Cependant, un moment, je fus gravement inquiet : la rouille avait rempli les tailles, je ne pouvais plus fuivre l'effet du mordant ! Un homme du métier que je confultai dut me donner un remède fcabreux que j'eus le bon efprit d'appliquer convenablement, et je fauvai ma planche de ce pas fi difficile. Pendant une bonne partie de l'opération j'avais travaillé à l'aveuglette. Ne voyant pas ce que fe paffait fous le mordant, j'avais augmenté progreffivement la dofe d'acide nitrique jufqu'à une forte proportion. Quand j'enlevai le vernis, je vis avec un contentement extrême que la morfure était convenablement graduée ; mais les tailles reftaient complétement obftruées de rouille. Ce même homme de l'art à qui je m'étais adreffé d'abord eut l'extrême bonté de me le dégager avec une extrême netteté. . . . Pour la terminer, je teintai, tant avec l'eau-forte d'abord, qu'enfuite à la pointe fèche, toutes les parties que le demandaient, et je fis auffi le ciel. En dernier lieu feulement j'ajoutai les deux portraits qui figurent à droite et à gauche dans le centre du cartouche.'

1ft St. Before any lettering, and before a confiderable amount of frefh working throughout.

2nd St. In the Rev. J. J. Heywood's collection, with the title and the initials of the bankers, but with one of their heads erafed, as if fault having been found with it, it was to be redrawn.

3rd St. With the title and publication line.

The fteel on which this magnificent, yet extraordinary defign was drawn is ftill in exiftence.   *w.* 39$\frac{1}{8}$ in. *h.* 9$\frac{1}{2}$ in.

23. 'VIEW OF THE RUINS OF THE CHÂTEAU OF
PIERREFONDS.'

This facfimile of a fketch from nature of Monfieur E. Viollet
le Duc, was etched by Méryon during his firft confinement in the
afylum at Charénton.

1ft-St. Before much fubfequent working on the plate in dry
point.

2nd St. With thefe additions.   *w.* 8⅛ in. *h.* 5⅞ in.

24. *Rue Pirouette-aux-Halles.*

This plate, which is remarkable even amongft Méryon's work,
for the elegance of the drawing with the needle, and the delicacy
of its biting, was executed after a drawing by an artift unknown
to fame, Monfieur Laurence. Méryon being at that time a prey
to melancholy, dreaded to work in the ftreets. He here gave the
exact outlines and effect of light and fhade, but drew from imagination the people who throng the ftreets of this popular and populous
quarter. ♦

He ufed the burin in this plate to a confiderable degree.

Trial Proof. Before the fky ; in pure etching.

1ft St. With the fky, and the effect of light, but before any
lettering.

2nd St., of which 20 impreffions were ftruck off. With
'*Rue Pirouette*, 1860,' the initials '*C. M. et L.*' on a chimney, and
the following fragments of an infcription on a wall, '*Jamet Md.
Marée : Bains de mer, Dieppe ; à Jeanne D'Arc outils lab.,*' etc.

3rd St. With the words, '*Laurence del — Méryon fculp.—
Delâtre imp. r. St. J.* 265 ;' and the infcription, '*Aux noces de*

Cana, Martingal reftaur feftins mariages repas. Au Diable Maure, Fortier Md. de Vins.'
4th St. With thefe differences in the infcriptions : '*Aux noces de Gamache, Sacoche, trait. Coufin, Md. de Vins, etc.'*
There are intermediate trial proofs, between thefe marked ftates, with very flight differences apparent in their work.
The copper is in exiftence.   *h.* 5 in. *w.* 4½ in.

25. 'PRESENTATION TO KING LOUIS XI. OF THE WORK VALÈRE MAXIME, PRINTED AT PARIS ABOUT 1475.'

Méryon executed with loving care this facfimile of a drawing in miniature, which belonged to M. Niel, Librarian to the Miniftry of the Interior.   .

The fcene depicted is a curious one : the king feated in a chair of ftate, furmounted by a canopy ornamented with fleurs-de-lys, accepts with hauteur the volume which is refpectfully prefented to him by a black-robed and bareheaded fubject. The courtiers intereft themfelves in various degrees in the ceremony. The view from the windows of the room is over a well-wooded landfcape.

Various trial proofs before the dry point work.

1ft St.   Recognifable by an accidental fcratch of the burin over the dreffes of the courtiers on the left.

2nd St.   The plate finifhed, but before the monogram ' *C. M.*' to the right of a page, which conftitutes the mark of a 4th ftate.

The plate is in exiftence.   *w.* 7⅞ in. *h.* 6¾ in.

26. *Chevet de S.ᵗ Martin-ſur-Renelle, Égliſe paroiſſiale ſup-primée en 1791*

This etching is a facſimile of a drawing of ' Polydes Langlois,' the Norman architect, antiquary, and critic.

Trial proof in pure etching.

1ſt St. With the words, ' *Polydes Langlois, 1837 — C. M., 21 Octobre, 1860 Imp.—Delâtre imp. des Feuillantines, 4.*'

2nd St. With the addition at the top of the plate, ' *Mémoires de la Société des Antiquaires de Normandie, t.* xxiv.'

h. 7⅛ in. w. 4⅞ in.

---

27. *Paſſerelle du Pont au Change après l'incendie de 1621 (d'après un deſſin du temps — tiré de la collection de Mr. Bonnardot) — Gazette des Beaux Arts. Imp. Delâtre, r. des Feuillantines, 4, Paris.*

1ſt St.   Before the initials ' *C. M.*' and before a boy ſtretched at full length on the ground to the left.

2nd St.   Same as 1ſt ſtate, except that the top marginal line is lightly drawn in.

3rd St.   Same as 2nd, but with the addition of a ſtump appearing to the left of a tree on the right.

4th St.   Before the title, with ' *C. M.*' at the bottom of the tree.   On ſome proofs the ſtamp of the collection Lagoy (an ' L ' in a triangle), which was ſubſequently effaced by the burniſher, appears to the right of the initials ' *C. M.*'

5th St.   With the title.   Struck off for the number of the *Gazette des Beaux Arts* which appeared on the 1ſt Nov. 1860. Printed on ordinary India paper and mounted.   The plate illuſtrated an intereſting article of M. Jules Couſin, now Librarian to the City of Paris.   Some trial proofs have the title without the addreſs of the printer.

6th St.   The title, '*Paſſerelle du Pont au Change, &c.*' which had been in italics, has reappeared in ſmall capitals.

The copper is in exiſtence.   *w.* 9 in. *h.* 4¾ in.

28. *Partie de la Cité de Paris, vers la fin du XVIIe. Siècle,
fur la rive gauche de la Seine, entre le Pont N^{e.} Dame et le
Pont au Change. N.B. Suivant toute probabilité la façade
méridionale des préfentes maifons, habitées par des Tanneurs,
formait un côté de la rue de la Pelleterie. Chofe affez fingulière,
par des caufes fur lefquelles peut f'exercer la fagacité des
curieux, des parties importantes du fujet, à favoir les Tours
Notre Dame, le coin de la pompe N^{e.} D^{e.} les cheminées des
pignons du Pont, manquent dans l'original, du moins le feul
emplacement eft indiqué ; tandis que les détails (que la gravure
a d'ailleurs foigneufement reproduits) y font faits avec minutie.
Enfin, pour rendre la vie à ces lieux le graveur a cru pouvoir
ajouter differents groupes de figures. (Le deffin fait partie de
la collection de Mr. Bonnardot.) Chez Rochoux, quai de
l'Horloge, 19.—Delâtre imp. r. de Feuillantines 2, Paris.*

The ftates of this plate would be no lefs than nine if one
accepted as fuch mere alterations in the foregoing legend as, for
inftance, ' *Rocheux* ' for ' *Rochoux*.' But it is not neceffary to
defcend to fuch puerilities, as every one will agree that differences
of ftate fhould be real differences in the defign of the work. Of
fuch there are three, which are well determined and marked out.

1ft trial proof.   Before the fky and before the towers of
Notre Dame.

2nd trial proof.   The fky ftill unfinifhed on the left ; the
towers of Notre Dame inferted ; fmoke iffues from two large
chimneys on the right.

1ft St.   The words, '*Au Cana C. Méryon reftaura, Paris, an
de gra*, MDCCCLXI.' are to be found on the right on a large placard
which is affixed to the gable ends.

2nd St.   The words '*Au Cana*' are effaced. Impreffions of
this ftate, which is called the ' before letters ' ftate, were ftruck
off to the extent of 20.

3rd St.   The words which were on the placard in the 2nd
ftate are effaced, and in their ftead thefe, ' *Le fobre refta, Poiffons
fr. au Répu.*' One hundred impreffions of this ftate, which has
for its title the long legend which we have tranfcribed, having
been ftruck off the plate was deftroyed.

This etching afforded to Méryon's friends one of the moft
convincing proofs of his unfortunate malady. In fpite of their

counfels, and of the advice of Mons. Bonnardot, who wifhed him to keep to the original defign, Méryon pretended that the towers of Notre Dame, and the chimneys of the houfes, had been effaced in the original drawing by evil-difpofed perfons, and he infifted on placing them in his etching; thus tranfgreffing hiftorical accuracy with a perfiftency which could leave no doubt in any one's mind as to his mental condition.   *w.* 12⅜ in. *h.* 6 in.

29. *Le Grand Châtelet à Paris, d'après un deffin exécuté en 1780 ; faifant partie de la collection de M. Bérard. —C. M. fculp. 1861—Pierron imp. rue Montfaucon 1, chez Rochoux, quai de l'Horloge 19.*

Méryon executed this etching in rather too off-hand a manner, and without much attempt at refemblance, from an Indian ink fketch attributed to Nicolle.

1ft St.   Before the working in the fky and on the ftaircafe in the centre.

2nd St.   Before any lettering.   Twenty proofs were taken of this ftate.

3rd St.   With the lettering.   The plate was broken up after one hundred impreffions had been ftruck off.   *w.* 11¾ in. *h.* 9¼ in.

30. *Vue de l'ancien Louvre du côté de la Seine, 1651.*
    Ch. Méryon d'après Zeeman.

This plate, which Méryon etched with care but in a heavy manner after a picture in the Louvre, was completed but a short time before his second and final entrance into the Asylum at Charenton.

1st St.   Before any lettering.
2nd St.   With above title.

The copper of this etching is in the Calchographie Nationale at the Louvre.   *w.* 10½ in. *h.* 6½ in.

31. *Eaux-fortes sur Paris, par C. Méryon,* MDCCCLII.

The title, printed on the grey cover of Méryon's principal work, *Eaux-fortes sur Paris.* The etching represents a block of limestone, with shell-marks and the imprint of moss deeply imbedded in it, and was intended to be typical of the foundations of Paris, the original specimen having been taken from the quarries of Montmartre. The title is engraved on the surface of the block in fanciful letters.

There is but one state of this.   *h.* 6¼ in. *w.* 4¾ in.

The set of *Eaux-fortes sur Paris* consist of—

THE TITLE (31).
FOUR SETS OF VERSES (32, 34, 49, and 51).
TWO FRONTISPIECES (33 and 46).
TWELVE PRINCIPAL ETCHINGS, viz. :—

Le Stryge (37).
Le Petit Pont (38).
L'Arche du Pont Notre Dame (39).
La Galerie de Notre Dame (40).
Le Tour de l' Horloge (42).
Tourelle, rue de la Tixéranderie (43).

Saint Etienne du Mont (44).
La Pompe Notre Dame (45).
Le Pont Neuf (47).
Le Pont au Change (48).
La Morgue (50).   [(52).
L'Abside de Notre Dame de Paris

TWO MINOR ETCHINGS OF THE ARMS OF PARIS (35 and 36).

AND TWO TAILPIECES :—
    The Rue des Mauvais Garçons (41).
    Le Tombeau de Molière (53).

IN ALL 23 ETCHINGS.

32. *À Reinier, dit Zeeman,** *peintre et eau-fortier.* *C. Méryon fecit,* MDCCCLIV. *Imp. Rue Neuve-St.-Etienne-du-Mont, No. 26.*

Verfes, in number forty-two, were etched on a few proofs. They commence—

> '*Peintre des matelots!*
> *Toi dont la main calleufe.*
> *En ta verve amoureufe*
> *Par de fi fimples traits*
> *Sut dire les attraits*
> *De la mer et des flots.*
> *De ce premier ouvrage,*
> *Où j'ai gravé Paris,*
> *La Ville à la Galère*
> *Qu' à ton inftar je fis*
> *En ta fimple manière,*
> *Accepte au moins l'hommage.*'

> . . . .

We confine ourfelves to citing thefe two ftanzas. The whole formed a fort of poetical ornament which the public failed to appreciate or underftand.

There is only one ftate of this. *h.* 6⅞ in. *w.* 2¾ in.

---

* It was, as we have before ftated, Zeeman's work, *The Pavilion of Mademoifelle* (No. 8) which firft gave Méryon the idea of etching a feries of Views of Paris.

33. ' OLD GATEWAY OF THE PALAIS DE JUSTICE,'
Paris. C. Méryon f.it. MDCCCLIV. *Imp. rue Nᵉ.-St.-Etienne-
du-Mont,* Nᵒ. *26.*

The frontiſpiece of the work. An imp unfurls a banneret on
which can with difficulty be deciphered, ' *Eaux-fortes ſur Paris
par Méryon.*' He hovers over the old gate of the Palais de Juſtice,
on which is engraved, ' PARIS, MDCCCL–I–IV.'   Its maſſive
towers are vigorouſly drawn, as well as the further roofs of the
city ; the whole being encircled by fantaſtic rays.

1ſt St.   Before the publication line, and printed on the ſame
plate as the ' *Tombeau de Molière,*' the ſize being *h.* 6¼ in. *w.* 5½ in.
Mr. Haden has a proof in this ſtate.

2nd St.   The copper cut, but before any lettering.

3rd St.   With the publication line etched in a circle of
which the diameter is 3⅜ in.

34. *Qu'âme pure rougiſſe.*

Méryon had engraved, to accompany the foregoing etching, a ſcore of verſes, commencing—

> ' *Qu'âme pure rougiſſe*
> *Mais ci pour frontiſpiece*
> *Je prends noir diablotin*
> *Malicieux, mutin*
> *Dominant de ſes ailes*
> *Les vieilles tours jumelles*
> *De la cité Paris.*'
> . . . .

At the bottom the publication line, ' *C. M.* MDCCCLIV. *Méryon imp. Rue Neuve-Sᵗ.-Etienne-du-Mont, No. 26.*' An alteration, neceſſitated by the abſurdity of the heart bluſhing, was afterwards made, and the word *gemiſſe* took the place of *rougiſſe* in the firſt line. A few proofs were ſtruck off and the copper was deſtroyed.

h. 2⅞ in. *w.* 1¾ in.

We may here make a remark which will aſſiſt amateurs in their ſearch for ' firſt ſtates.' Méryon lit upon ſeveral quires of vergé paper, very thin and green in colour; on this paper he ſtruck off his trial proofs and thoſe compriſing his ' firſt ſtates,' and this paper gave to them a remarkably powerful and original effect, though they were as a whole heavy through too much loading with ink. At that time the Japaneſe paper, which now enables ſuch brilliant tirages to be taken, was but little known. The beſt proofs of Méryon's works were originally taken off by Auguſte Delàtre, on a beautiful Dutch vergé paper, which was ſlightly diſcoloured by age. In his youth this clever printer produced from the preſs chefs-d'œuvre of the printer's art, and his name will be inſeparably connected with the revival of etching in France and England.

35. ' ARMS SYMBOLICAL OF THE CITY OF PARIS.'

C. Méryon f^t. MDCCCLIV. *Imp. Rue N^e. S^t. Etienne du Mont*, 26.

The field of the fhield is ftrewn with lilies in three bands. A galley in full fail floats on a calm fea. She fhapes her courfe to the right, which is contrary to the rules of heraldry. She was copied from a galley, carved in a ftone bas-relief at Bourges, of the date of the middle ages. A mural crown, formed of gateways and fquare towers, crenellated and connected by ramparts, furmounts the fhield, which is fupported by branches of olive and oak.

Trial proof before any letters and before the copper was cut, the fize being, *h.* 6⅓ in. *w.* 5½ in.

1ft St.   With the publication line.   *h.* 5¼ in. *w.* 4½ in.

36. *Fluctuat nec mergitur.*   *C. M.*   MDCCCLI–IV.

A galley, fymbolical of the city of Paris, preffes forward with fwelling fail and pulfating oars. The crown which furmounts the efcutcheon is compofed of cannon, mouths downwards, connected by a folid wall, and fupported by a band of cannon-balls in imitation of pearls. Méryon never obtained the requifite authority from the Minifter of the Interior to publifh this magnificent etching, which feemed to hint at the terrorifm of the Empire, and fo there exift but few impreffions.

The original pen-and-ink drawing is in Mr. Haden's collection. A woodcut from this etching appeared in the *Gazette des Beaux Arts* of 1864, and it was fubfequently printed on the cover of the ' *Paris Guide, par les principaux écrivains et artiftes de la France, 1867.*' It differs from the etching and original drawing in that the oars are uplifted inftead of being played.

There is but one ftate.   *h.* 6⅝ in. *w.* 6¼ in.

37. *Le Stryge. C. M. No. 1, Delâtre imp. rue Saint Jacques, 265.*

This plate reprefents one of the carved figures which adorn the angles of the towers of Notre Dame. The Stryge, the upper half of his body only feen, refts his head in his hands and contemplates the city which unfolds itfelf beneath him.

Trial proof. Before the figure of the Stryge and the tower of St. Jacques.

1ft St. The plate finifhed, and with the initials ' *C. M.*' on a chimney near the bottom of the etching.

2nd St. Publication line inferted thus: on one fide, '*C. Méryon del. et fculp.*,' and the date ' MDCCCLIII.' reverfed; on the other fide, '*A Delâtre imp. rue de la Bûcherie, 6.*' Beneath this two lines of verfe in the ftyle of the poet Pierre Gringoire, written in Gothic charaĉters faithfully copied from a MS. of the 15th century.

> ' *Infatiable vampire, l'éternelle luxure.*
> *Sur la grande cité convoite fa pâture.*'

Near thefe the initials ' *C. M.*'

3rd St. The two lines of verfe have been effaced.

4th St. Laft tirage made by Méryon after his releafe from Charenton. He retouched this and all the plates of the fet with the burin (which made them darker than in the earlier ftates), took off fome 30 impreffions, and deftroyed them. With the title,* the above publication line, and alfo '*A Delâtre imprimeur rue Saint Jacques, 265.*'   *h.* 6¾ in. *w.* 5⅛ in.

---

* The Britifh Mufeum impreffion of this ftate has only the title and no other lettering.

38. *Le Petit Pont.*

This view is taken from the towing-path at the foot of the Quai de la Tournelle. The towers of Notre Dame, which rear themſelves in the upper part of the compoſition, are much too high, regard being had to their real dimenſions and the laws of perſpective. We ſhould be called upon in ſeveral inſtances to draw attention to errors of this nature were they not entirely voluntary ones, and on the whole permiſſible. Méryon never pretended that his plates had the cold exactitude of a photograph. When he took his firſt ſketch from below—from the water's edge, for inſtance—it is evident he placed himſelf in a poſition which, if reproduced, would have been unrecogniſable to the majority of ſpectators. He mounts, therefore, to the bank, and with a facility almoſt unequalled tacks on to his firſt idea the view which uſually ſtruck the paſſer-by from the parapet. By theſe two operations he compoſed a picture which at the ſame time is a real view. Mr. Haden poſſeſſes ſome very careful drawings of the Towers of Notre Dame: they are inſcribed in Méryon's writing, ‘*Deſſins ayant ſervi pour le Petit Pont. C. M. 1850.*’

1ſt St. Before the marginal line at the bottom and the initials ‘ *C. M.*’ in the upper right corner.

2nd St. Finiſhed, with the initials, but before any lettering, and before the bottom marginal line. Some dry point ſcratching on the left bottom margin.

3rd St. The ſame, but with the dry point marks removed.

4th St. With the title and theſe words, ‘ *Publié par l'Artiſte*’ written with the needle. The ſky is lowered in tone by diagonal downward ſtrokes from right to left.

5th and laſt St. With the number ‘ *2*,’ the title, ‘ *Le Petit Pont, 1850*,’ reinſcribed in little capitals, and ‘ *Delâtre imp. Rue Sᵗ. Jacques, 265.*’ Méryon in this ſtate ‘reduced what to him ſeemed the too violent oppoſition of the black and white by dry point working.’ *   h. 9⅝ in. w. 7¼ in.

---

* The remarks here and elſewhere placed within inverted commas were furniſhed by Méryon himſelf to Mr. Burty, when he was compiling the firſt catalogue of his work.

39. *L'Arche du pont Notre-Dame, 1850.*

Underneath the arch of the Bridge are feen the piles which uphold the '*pompe à feu;*' further, the Pont au Change and the towers of the Palace de Juftice. This was the firft of the feries executed by Méryon. He availed himfelf of the *chambre claire*, but he was obliged to entirely remodel the defign which this inftrument had furnifhed him with.

Trial proof, in pure etching. ·Thefe proofs are very rare : Méryon, finding that they did not exprefs his feelings, deftroyed them in almoft every inftance, whenever he could lay hands upon them.

1ft St. With crofs-hatching on the under-fide of the arch.

2nd St. With, to the left, '*C. Méryon, del. fculp. imp. rue N°· S¹· Etienne du Mont 26*'—to the right, '*Paris, 1853.*'

3rd and laft St. With the title, '*No. 3,*' in left bottom corner, and the words—which appear in all his laft printings—'*A. Delâtre imp. R. S¹· Jacques 265.*' In the upper angle the initials '*C. M.*' 'Delicate corrections with the burin. The dry point work in the fky, which diftinguifhes the earlier ftates, has almoft difappeared.'

w. 7¾ in. *h.* 6 in.

40. *La Galerie de Notre-Dame.*

Jackdaws are building in the Gallery. Through the fine Gothic colonnade, as Victor Hugo, in his *Notre-Dame de Paris*, fays, 'the eye dwells on a maze of roofs, chimneys, ftreets, bridges, fquares, fpaces, and towers ; and fpecially towards the Weft on the Palais de Juftice, fettled down on the borders of the river midft its group of towers.'

Trial proof in Mr. Haden's colleétion (with ftatement on its face that it was printed by Méryon) before the infertion of the fhaded fky above the cumuli, and with the upper of the two jackdaws who fly between the two colonnades almoft white. The whole in pure etching.

1ft St. The jackdaw is now black. Additional bitings have already lowered the wonderful aërial effeét of the trial proof.

2nd St. Finifhed and with ' *C. Méryon, del. Jculp. 1853. Imp. rue N°· S¹·-Etienne-du-Mont, 26.*'

3rd St. With the addrefs which appeared in the laft ftate erafed, and in its place the monogram ' *C. M.*' in the upper left corner ; five Jackdaws have been added between the two laft columns to the right, and this title, '*la Galerie N***D.*'

4th and laft St. With the number '*4*,' the addiefs, '*A. Delatre, R. S¹· Jacques, 265.*' 'Le clocheton de la tourelle qui occupe la partie centrale du fond a été refait.'

We may ftate here that in all thefe laft, numbered, ' tirages ' retouches have been made with the burin.   *h.* 11 in. *w.* 6⅞ in.

41. 'THE RUE DES MAUVAIS-GARÇONS.'

Houfes built in many courfes, and pierced by irregular openings, which are guarded by thick iron bars : one of the houfes, which is protected againft vehicles by enormous ftone ftruts, bears in large characters above the door the number '*12*.' Two women pafs along, one of whom carries a bundle on her arm. The compofition is fingularly powerful. It quietly fhows that antithefis fo often to be met with in the old quarters of great towns, the fun enlivening at certain times the fœtid runnel, and gilding the walls of the unfavoury hovel. This view formed the tail-piece of the firft part of the *Eauxfortes fur Paris*.

1ft St. Before the verfes, with the infcription '*Méryon imp. rue Neuve-Saint-Etienne-du-Mont, 26*,' and with an '*M*.' in dry point on the left hand ftone ftrut.

2nd St. With thefe verfes :—

'*Quel mortel habitait*   '*Etait-ce la vertu*
En ce gite fi fombre?   *Pauvre, filencieufe?*
Qui donc là fe cachait   *Le Crime diras-tu*
Dans la nuit et dans l'ombre? *Ou quelqu'âme haineufe.*

'*Ah! ma foi, je l'ignore.*
Si tu veux le favoir,
Curieux, vas y voir.
Il en eft temps encore.'

PARIS, Mars . . . LIV.

h. 4⅞ in. *w.* 3⅞ in.

42. *La Tour de l'Horloge.*

The Pont au Change, under an arch of which a loaded barge paſſes, croſſes the compoſition : to the left the Palais de Juſtice, whoſe buildings ſtretch along the Quai des Orfèvres.

Trial proof in pure etching.

1ſt St.   Before the marginal line at the bottom and before the dry point work in the ſky.

2nd St.   The plate finiſhed, but before the initials ' *C. M.*' in the right top corner.

3rd St.   With the initials ' *C. M.*'   Mr. Haden has an impreſſion which would appear to come between this and the foregoing ſtate, it having no marginal line.

4th St.   With the title and ' *publié par l'Artiſte,*' and the addreſs of the printer, ' *Imp. Aug. Delâtre, R. S. Jacque, 171.*'

5th and laſt St.   With the monogram, the number ' *5,*' and the ſame title re-engraved in little capitals ; the triangular roof of the Tour de l'Horloge, white in the preceding ſtates, is ſhaded in this.

' The middle diſtance has been worked up.   The old building, which is in courſe of demolition, affords a paſſage through its windows to two gleams of light, which, coming from behind, let daylight into the centre of the compoſition, which in the earlier ſtates was too uniformly black and wanting in intereſt.   In various parts, particularly at the top of the ſcaffolding, ſmall figures have been added.   On the parapet of the bridge many modifications have been made.   Laſtly, in the right diſtance, one of the ſemicircular ſhops of the Pont Neuf, which was in the way, has been removed ſo as to allow the clumps of trees on the river bank to be ſeen to greater advantage.'

An impreſſion of this ſtate in the Britiſh Muſeum bears the words, ' Bon à tirer quinze épreuves, C. M.'   *h.* 10¼ in. *w.* 7⅛ in.

43. *Tourelle, rue de la Tixéranderie, démolie en 1851.* C. M.

Two perfons leaning back againft an iron railing, point to the tower built at the angle of the Rue du Coq. A Soldier paffes on horfeback.

1ft St. Before the letters '*C. M.*' in the upper right corner.

2nd St. Before the title, and with the initials '*C. M.*'

3rd and laft St. With number '6,' the title, and '*A. Delâtre imp. R. S*ᵗ*. Jacques, 265.*' 'The upper portion of the vine, which is in the fhade, has been worked up.'   h. 9⅜ in. w. 5¼ in.

44. *Saint-Etienne-du-Mont.*

The central portion of the portico of the Church is feen between the buildings (already pulled down) of the ancient College de Montaigu and the angle of the Pantheon.

1ft Trial Proof in pure etching, the plate is about 11¼ inches high by 6⅓ wide. In the Rev. J. J. Heywood's Collection.

2nd Trial Proof. The plate reduced in fize.

1ft St. The plate has been rebitten and touched up with the burin throughout, the initials '*C. M.*' inferted in the right top corner.

2nd St. The workman, who on the bottom ftage of the fcaffolding reaches out to receive a pole, has his arms erafed.

3rd St. In the top corner of the angle of the Pantheon the words, '*St. Ene.-du-Mont.—Bibliothéque Sainte-Geneviève.*'

4th and laft St. With the number '7.' The work on the façade of the Church is finifhed by harmonifing the tones. At the top of the picture to the right, the title : '*Saint-E*ⁿᵉ*.-du-Mont et l'ancien collége de Montaigu,*' this laft title being the one to be applied to the edifice which forms the block on the left, and on which is written befide other notices, '*A. Delâtre, imprimeur taille-douce, eau-forte. R. S. Jacque, 265.*' The workman, before mentioned, has his arms wider apart, and his body fronting the fpectator.

N.B.—There is an eafily diftinguifhable copy of this plate in circulation.   *h.* 9¾ in. *w.* 5⅛ in.

45. *La Pompe Notre-Dame. 1852.**

The Pompe Notre-Dame and its picturefque piles occupy the centre of the compofition. On the right one fees the high towers of Notre Dame beyond the houfes on the quay.

Trial Proof. The fifhing-net left quite white.

1ft St. in pure etching. At the bottom, written in reverfed lettering, '*C. Méryon, ft. R. N^{a.}-St.-Etienne-du-Mont, 26.—1852.*'

2nd St. Touched up with the burin throughout, and the infcription of the firft ftate re-written the proper way: '*C. Meryon ft. Imp. R. N^{e.} St. Etienne du Mont, 26.—1852.*'

3rd St., with thefe words in addition: '*Publié par l'Artifte. La Pompe Notre-Dame. Imp^{e.} A. Delâtre, R. St.-Jacques, 176.*'

4th St. The title in capitals, the words '*Publié par l'artifte*' erafed, the Number '*8. C. Méryon, D. S.,*' in the upper right corner. The roofs, which are white in the preceding ftates, are here fhaded with dry point.

5th St. Same as preceding, but the word *Méryon* erafed fave the initial letter.   *w.* 10 in. *h.* 6¾ in.

---

* The date ufually refers to the time when the firft fketch from nature was taken.

46. ‘THE LITTLE PUMP.’ *Méryon.* *C. M. f. Imp. R. N^e*
St.-Etienne-du-Mont, 26.

Méryon compofed this elegant yet fpirited fantafy as a frontifpiece to the fecond part of the Paris Views.   At the top of the
compofition two dolphins fpout water through their noftrils ;
below, two pipes iffuing on either fide of the body of the pump,
rife in graceful curves, fuftain overflowing cups, interlace and
form circles in which are the letters ‘*P. N. D.*’ (Pompe Notre
Dame), and terminate in the form of the head of a fwan.   The
whole forms an oval framework for the following whimfica.
verfes :—

<table>
<tr><td>

‘ *C’en eft fait*
O forfait !
Pauvre pompe
Sans pompe
Il faut mourir !
</td><td>

‘ *Mais pour amoirir*
Cet arrêt inique
Par un tour bachique
Que ne pompes-tu
En impromptu.
</td></tr>
</table>

‘ *Au lieu d’eau claire*
Qu’on n’aime guère
— *Du vin*
— *Bien fin ?*—MDCCCLIV.’

1ft St.   Before the publication line and various workings.
There alfo exift trial proofs which fhow that the margin of the
copper had not been cleaned.

2nd St.   With infcription, and added working on the plate :
the pump fhaded, rays of light iffue from the letters *P. N. D* ,
and water flows from the cups.   *b.* 110 in. *w.* 80 in.

47. *Le Pont-Neuf.*

The fpeĉator is fuppofed to be ftanding at the water's edge.

Trial proof, in pure etching.

1ft St.   Before any letters, and before the marginal line at the bottom.

2nd St.   With the name and addrefs of the Printer written in an inverfe direĉtion.   The fky has been effaced, and the houfes in the diftance are indicated only in pencil.

3rd St.   Worked upon with the burin throughout.   With publication line, ' *C. Méryon del. fculp. 1853—Imp. A. Delâtre, rue de la Bucherie, No. 6.*'

4th St.   Same as laft ftate, but with eight verfes, of which the firft alone need be here reproduced.

> ' *Ci-gît du vieux Pont Neuf*
> *L'exaĉte refemblance,*
> *Tout radoubé de neuf,*
> *Par récente ordonnance. . . .*'

5th St.   A trial proof, probably unique.   The verfes have been rubbed off, and have not yet been replaced by the title, which appears in the following ftate.

6th St.   The chimney of the Mint, as well as the verfes, have difappeared.   The latter are replaced by the fimple title, '*Le Pont-Neuf,*' written with the needle.

7th and laft St.   With the number '*9*,' the initials '*C. M.*,' the title re-written in fmall capitals.   The houfes, which are feen above the femicircular fhops, have been entirely redrawn, and are much fmaller.   7¼ in. *fquare.*

48. *Le Pont au Change.*

The bridge, above which is feen the roof of the Pompe-à-feu, occupies the middle diftance ; to the right is the Palais de Juftice, beyond the trees on the Quai aux Fleurs.

Trial proof, before the fky, and the bottom and under part of the arches. Mr. Heywood has a trial proof with the Palais de Juftice and the bridge only.

1ft St. Before the rebiting in the background, and removal of traces of burr.

2nd St. Finifhed in pure etching. A balloon, bearing on its fide the word *Speranza*, rifes in the air amid the acclamations of the crowd on the bridge.

3rd St. Worked up throughout with the point, with the publication line, ' *C. Méryon, del. fculp.* MDCCCLIIII. *Imp. R. Neuve-S^t.-Etienne-du-Mont, 26.*'

4th St. With a number of fmall balloons, borne along by the wind. The monogram ' *C. M.*' on the left upper corner, and the title below the plate, ' *Le Pont au Change.*'

5th St. One day Méryon gave Mr. Burty a proof of this ftate before he had put in the birds. In the empty fpace in the fky he had drawn, with a very finely-pointed pencil, what his fancy, like Hamlet's, faw there : the clouds were formed of the flefhy forms of women recumbent and afleep; over one of them a ferpent hung his huge fnake-like coils, alfo combining to form the clouds. Above was depicted one of the Ifles of Polynefia, covered with lofty palm-trees. Towards this a chariot, as it might be that of the fun, afcended. A man alfo threw himfelf into fpace ; this Méryon gravely faid was ' le fort, qui attend le mortel, trop ambitieux.' Nothing could excel the originality and brightnefs of thefe luminous fpots in the darkened brain of this poet—acquired, however, only at rare intervals, and rarely taking a form which admitted of their being compofed into a harmonious whole.

At the fale of the Niel Collection, a proof of this ftate, probably a unique trial proof, with the clouds drawn in pencil, but without the foregoing mythological figures, was fold for 102 francs to Holloway and Sons of London.

F

6th St.   All the fky has been taken out.   It is now evening, and the crefcent of the new moon has been inferted.   A flight of albatrofles foar above a flock of wild duck, who fcatter themfelves in every direction.   Méryon was infected, even thus early, with an idea that, at the clofe of day, eagles and other birds of prey were let loofe from the Tuileries, whofe threatening flight carried trouble into the peaceful minds of the citizens, and recalled to them the triumph of the coup d'état of 1851.   With the title and monogram in the upper left corner.

7th St.   With the fky worked up, but before the final title.

8th St.   With the number ' *10* '—the monogram ' *C. M.*'   A cloud of air balloons bearing the titles, *Vafco de Gama*, *l'Afmodée*, *le Protée*, *le Saint Elme*, float in every direction.

This etching is one among many in Méryon's works where the air is as full of vitality as the earth, and where both in accord combine a gracefulnefs very rarely encountered in works of this clafs.   *w.* 13, *h.* 6⅜ in.

49. *L'Espérance.*

Méryon compofed a fet of verfes which embody his feelings with refpect to the foregoing plate. He etched them and ftruck off a few proofs. They bear as title *L'Espérance*, and are as follows :—

> ' *Léger aéroftat, ô divine Efpérance,*
> *Comme le frêle efquif que le houle balance*
> *Au fouffle nonchalant des paifibles auta s*
> *Pars, et dans les vapeurs que promènent les vents,*
> *Découvre-toi parfois à nos regards avides*
> *Sur le fond bleu du ciel, dans les régions placides,*
> *Où d'un riche foleil les rayons fécondants*
> *Tracent en lignes d'or tous les rèves brillants*
> *D'un douteux avenir . . .*
> *Mais, ô trifte rêveur, pourquoi dans les nuages*
> *Te promener ainfi ? . . .*
> *Reviens, reviens, à terre . . .*
> *Crains de tenter du Sort le caprice bizarre . . .*
> *Puifqu'un Deftin nouveau t'a mis la pointe en main,*
> *T'a fait paffer graveur de drop fièle marin,*
> *Vas ! que fur l'endroit noir qui recourre ton cuivre*
> *Ta main laiffe après toi le remous qui doit fuivre*
> *Tout efquif paffager fur l'orageufe mer*
> *Qu'on appelle le Vie, ocean dur, amer,*
> *Où trop fouvent, hélas ! fallacieux mirage,*
> *L'efpoir qui nous leurrait va mourir au rivage.*
>
> C. M., *Mars* MDCCCLIV.

Méryon made a few unimportant variations in the foregoing, which might be faid to conftitute a fecond ftate did they occur in a picture, and not in what only takes the place of a printed document.   *h.* 2½ in. *w.* 5 in.

50. *La Morgue, 1850.*

This etching is one of Méryon's moſt powerful works—one in which is moſt eminently viſible his power of inſtilling poetry and piċturefquenefs into the moſt unintereſting ſcene. It need hardly here be mentioned that the Morgue is the building to which are taken all the corpſes found in the highways, in the river, and in untenanted houfes. The old building had nothing remarkable in itſelf; but Méryon has imparted to it an imperifh-able charaċter, by his rigid drawing of the principal lines, his potent contraſts of light and ſhade, and by the addition of a drama of the moſt realiſtic charaċter. How full of myſtery are the three figures,—the corpfe juſt dragged from the river, the woman overcome with defpair, the fobbing child! From a technical point of view, too, this plate is a chef d'œuvre,—the copper has been attacked by the needle with a furenefs of hand, and the plate has been bitten with a freedom and certainty of ſuccefs which is moſt remarkable. Everything throughout the work is powerful and expreſſive, and leaves nothing to be defired.

1ſt trial proof, in pure etching. The Sergent-de-ville, who points to the building—the group of lookers-on—the corpfe which is being carried along—the ſmoke which iſſues from the chimneys—are indicated but not modelled.

2nd trial proof. Before any lettering.. Before the marginal line is finifhed at the top left corner, and with a white ſpot left behind the man who ſtands on the parapet.

1ſt St. Finifhed before any lettering.

2nd St. To the left, '*C. Méryon del. fculp.* MDCCCLIV.' To the right, '*Imp. Rue Neuve-St.-Etiénne-du-Mont, No. 26.*'

3rd St. The number *11*, the monogram '*C. M.*', correċtions made in the drawing of the corpfe. Sign-boards poſted up on the buildings, '*Hôtel des Trois-Balances. Sabra, dentiſte du peuple.*' '*Mots dans la confonnance ou la fécrete fignification,*' wrote Méryon, '*femble s'harmonifer avec ces lieux d'un caractère plein d'auſtérité.*'

4th St. Before deſtroying this plate, Méryon added yet this infcription to the houfe loweſt down in the picture, '*Imagerie, religieufe, exportation.*'   *h.* 9⅛ in. *w.* 8⅛ in.

51. *L'Hôtellerie de la Mort.*

Méryon engraved on two fmall plates, from which he printed a few proofs in two colours, the following ftanzas, which are imbued with a profound melancholy and a confiderable amount of eloquence. They refer to the foregoing plate of the Morgue.

'Venez, voyez, paffants !
A fes pauvres enfants
En mère charitable,
La Ville de Paris
Donne en tous temps gratis,
Et le lit et la table.

Regardez fans pâlir
Ces faces impaffibles,
Souriantes, terribles,
Enigmes d'avenir . . . .

Ici la Mort couvie
Tous ceux que, par deftin,
Couchent fur les chemins
Amour, Mifère, Envie.

. . . . .

Paffants, paffants, priez
Pour tous les trépaffés
Qu'à la Mort envieufe

Amène fans tarir
La ville du Plaifir,
En ce monde fameufe !

. . . . .

Mais qui fait fi la Mort,
Sous fon mafque fevère,
Ne nous cache du Sort
Quelque riant myftère ?

Qui fait fi la Douleur,
En foulevant fon voile
Du terme du labeur
Ne nous montre l'étoile?

Allez, pauvres humains,
Creufez, fouillez la terre
De vos pieds, de vos mains !
Il faut à la Mifére
Chaque jour fa pain-noir.' . .

h. 4⅞ in. *w.* 1⅝ in.

52. L'Abſide de Notre Dame de Paris.

The towers of the Cathedral, ſeen from the foot of the Pont de la Tournelle, dominate the nave and its buttreſſes. To the left the three arches of the Pont aux Choux ſpan the river, and beyond are ſeen the ancient buildings of the Hôtel Dieu. This view of Notre Dame is ſtrikingly majeſtic. The Cathedral, which inſpired a poet to write one of the moſt beautiful works of our generation, appears to have exerciſed a great influence over Méryon's dreamy ſpirit, and to it we owe his lovelieſt plate. It is alſo the one which has called for the exerciſe of the greateſt amount of knowledge of drawing, of compoſition, and of taſte. For it muſt be remembered that photography had not then placed in the hands of artiſts reductions of views, whereby they could obtain either tracings or valuable hints. Note well how Méryon has preſerved in his drawing of this Gothic building all the vaſt-neſs and elegance of proportion which are the characteriſtic types of that branch of French architecture. Méryon wrote on a few of the early proofs of this plate, one of which is in Mr. J. Fiſher's Collection, the following lines :—

> '*O toi déguſtateur de tout morceau gothique*
> *Vois ici de Paris la noble baſilique*
> *Nos Rois, grands et dévôts, ont voulu la bâtir.*
> *Pour témoigner au maître un profond repentir.*
> *Quoique bien grand, hélas! on la dit trop petite*
> *De nos moindres pécheurs pour contenir l'élite.*'

1ſt trial proof. Before the ſky and the buildings of the Hôtel Dieu on the left. A variation of this is in Mr. Heywood's Collection.

2nd trial proof. Before the completion of the upper marginal line and the ſky to the right.

1ſt St. Completed, but ſtill before additions in dry point to the ſky to the right, and with marks of the vice on the margin.

2nd St. The plate cleaned, and the publication line, '*C.*

Méryon, del. fculp. MDCCCLIV. *Imp. Rue neuve Sᵗ· Etienne du Mont 26.'*

3rd St. Same as laſt ſtate, but with the title written with the needle.

4th St. With the number '*12*,' the monogram '*C. M.*' The title rewritten in ſmall capitals, followed by the date, '*1853.*'

5th St. With '*Méryon, del. fculp.*' in the upper left angle.

w. 11½ in. *h.* 6 in.

53. *Le Tombeau de Molière.*

We have failed to diſcover what idea poſſeſſed Méryon in chooſing, as a tail-piece to the ſet of views of Paris, the tomb at Père la Chaiſe of the great ſatiriſt, Molière. On a plinth which ſuſtains a flaming urn is placed the name '*Molière.*' Beneath, the galley, which Paris has taken for her heraldic arms, appears as a ſeal on the knot of the crown of laurels with which this enigmatical but ſuggeſtive compoſition is ſurrounded.

Trial proof on the ſame copper as the '*Old Gate of the Palais de Juſtice*' (No. 33).

1ſt and only State. With the title and publication line, '*C. Méryon, fᵗ·* MDCCCLIV. *Imp. R. Nᵉ· Sᵗ· Etienne du Mont, Nᵒ· 26.*'

The copperplate was given by Méryon to his printer, A. Delâtre, and is in exiſtence. *w.* 2⅙ in. *h.* 2¾ in.

DIVISION No. III.

Isolated Views of Paris, Souvenirs of Travels to Bourges, New Zealand, and the Antipodes.

---

64. *Estampes anciennes, Rochoux, Quai de l'Horloge, No. 19.*

This charming book-plate was etched for M. Rochoux, the printseller, in two colours, red and black, by means of two coppers. In the upper portion the Seine and Marne are seated, with their backs to the Gothic doorway of the Palais de Justice; in the lower part is the equestrian statue of Henri IV. on the platform of the Pont Neuf.

1st trial proof, in pure etching. The lamp is placed on a white stand.

2nd trial proof. The lamp stands out against the shadow of the arch of the bridge, which is modelled.

1st St. The lamp is replaced by the galley, symbolical of the City of Paris.

2nd St. The cables, which form a sort of framework for the composition, are knotted at the lower angles. *w.* 4⅜ in. *h.* 3⅞ in.

55. *Tourelle, Rue de l'École-de-Médecine 22, Paris.*

Trial proof, in pure etching. Before the fky and before the words ' *Fiat lux* ' on the book.

1ft St.   Before the word ' *Mabat.*'

2nd St.   Before the two women feated in front of a laundrefs's cart.

3rd St.   Still no fky. The upper boundary line is curved ·in the middle, and in the arch are the monogram ' *C. M.*' and the words ' *Innocence opprimée* ' beneath the figure of a child, who hides her face and whofe wings have been pulled off. Lower ftill, LA VÉRITÉ defcends from heaven, holding a book whofe pages bear thefe words, '*Fiat lux ;*' whilft ' LA JUSTICE,' enveloped in clouds, lets fall her fcales and fword. In the ftreet below a hurried crowd follow their occupation, two mafons ftanding on a houfe-top above appearing to fee the vifion. Mr. Haden has a proof of this ftate numbered 3, and dated 31 Mars. 61.

4th St. has thefe words in the lower margin : ' *Tourelle dite de Marat.   Sainte, inviolable Vérité, divin flambeau de l'âme ; quand le chaos eft fur la terre, tu defcends des cieux pour éclairer les hommes, et régler les décrets de la ftriête Juftice.*'

5th St.   The allegorical figures have been erafed, but the two birds which replace them have not yet been inferted.

6th St.   The legend which appears in the 4th ftate has been erafed and a fky inferted, the title printed below, and ' *Imp. Reuon, r. Montfaucon 1, Paris.*'

· 7th St.   Two birds and the monogram in the fky ; the title, the date, ' MDCCCLXI.', and ' *Gazette des Beaux-Arts.*'

h. 8¼ in. *w.* 7 in.

Mr. Haden has the original fketch for this etching and a moft careful ftudy for the finial of the Turret. He has alfo an impreffion in which the clouds are worked up in pencil, and one of them is formed into the head of Charlotte Corday. It bears a date in Méryon's writing, ' *27 Juin.*' It was in the houfe with the turret that Marat was affaffinated.

56. *Rue de Chantres, Paris,* MDCCCLXII.

1ſt St., in pure etching, before the ſky, the birds in the air, and the animal at the top of the belfry ſpire of Notre Dame.

2nd St. Before the margin has been cleaned, and before the bells which ornament the top.

3rd St. Finiſhed, with two bells and the letters ' *J. B.*' in an arch at the top, but before any lettering.

4th St. With the title and theſe addreſſes : ' *Chez Rochoux, Quai de l'Horloge 19. Pierron, imp. r. Montfaucon 1.*'

This plate was deſtroyed after one hundred impreſſions had been taken off. A proof was hung in the Salon of 1863, but without attracting the attention of the Jury, any more than had any of Méryon's previous exhibits. *h.* 11¾ in. *w.* 5⅞ in.

57. CARVED DOORWAY TO AN OLD HOUSE AT BOURGES.

This plate was etched in 1851—that is to ſay, at the outſet of Méryon's career—and is of very delicate workmanſhip. Very few impreſſions were ever taken from it.

Mr. Haden ſaw Méryon at work on this etching in 1864. He had it fixed upright on an eaſel, and was delving upward ſtrokes in it with the burin.

1ſt St. In pure etching, before ſubſequent working on the left.

2nd St. With working on the left. *h.* 6⅝ in. *w.* 4⅝ in.

58. *La Rue des Toiles, Bourges.*

A dark and winding ftreet, whofe houfes are in the pureft 14th and 15th century ftyles.

Trial proof, in pure etching.

1ft St. With '*C. M. del. fculp. 1853*,' and the addrefs, '*Rue Nᵉ· St.-Etienne-du-Mont, 26.*' To the left is feen a dog fcratching up fome filth, and the date '*1853*' has been placed on a chimney to the right.

2nd St. The name and addrefs and the dog are effaced.

3rd St. In the place of the dog, a young foldier, in the coftume of the Middle Ages, talks with two women.

4th St. With the title.

The copperplate was given by Méryon to his printer, Delâtre, who ftruck off a feries of impreffions for Mr. Woodward, for the *Fine Arts Review.*

The proof which Méryon fent to the Salon in 1853 was rejected by the Jury.

Méryon wrote to Mr. Burty *àpropos* of this, etching, which is fo thoroughly invefted with the fpirit of the Middle Ages,—'All the upper portions of the houfes are true to nature; the lower parts had, however, been fo disfigured by modern reftorations, that I obtained from other quarters of the town details which would beft accord with the upper ftories.'   *h.* 8½ in. *w.* 4¾ in.

59. *Ancienne Habitation à Bourges.*

The angle of this houſe—built, it is ſaid, by a muſician who had made his fortune—is formed by a threefold pillar carved in the form of a flageolet. A boy blows a trumpet near to two nuns who are talking to a prieſt.

Trial proof, in pure etching, before any trace of dry point work.

1ſt St. Before the initials ' *C. M.*' on the ground to the left. The diſtance between the plate-mark meaſures—in width, 5⅞ in., height, 10⅞ in.

2nd St. The front of the two laſt houſes has been covered with a vineſtock.

4th St. With the title, and in this condition publiſhed in the *Gazette des Beaux-Arts,* after an edition (a 3rd State) had been ſtruck off on Dutch paper for the ſubſcribers to the work.

h. 9½ in. *w.* 5¼ in.

60. *Le Pilote de Tonga.*

On the inner fide of a frame (in the upper angles of which can be read the initials ' *T. T.*', ftanding for the words ' *Tonga-Tabou*') is written in red and black lettering this fong, imitative of the iflanders of New Zealand :—

> ' *Nous partions de Tonga fur un navire de guerre; vient le pilote dans la frêle pirogue. Il eft prefque complètement nu. Fort et agile, en un faut il eft à bord; il va droit au commandant et le falue digne-ment. Le navire ouvre fes voiles au vent; vivement pouffé par la brife qui les gonfle, il donne dans l'étroite et dangereufe paffe! Debout fur un banc de quart, la tête haute, l'œil attentif, l'habile pilote indique de gefte la route de navire qui fe joue dans les récifs! Son attitude eft noble et fière: tout chez lui dénote l'affurance. Sa large poitrine, de teinte bafanée, brille au foleil comme un bouclier d'airain, fes longs cheveux flottent au vent . . . A bord tout fe tait; officiers et matelots l'admirent en filence . . . Et le navire marche, marche toujours. . . . Mais le voie f'agrandit . . . Déjà la houle de large clapote fous la proue . . . Hourra, vaillant pilote, hourra!—Le paffe eft franche—Pourfuis ta courfe, ô beau navire. devant nous f'ouvre l'Océan. A toi, merci, pilote de Tonga!* ' . . .

This fong, compofed in profe, after the manner of the inhabitants of New Zealand, was intended as a preface to a feries of fouvenirs of the voyage of the corvette *Rhine*, which Méryon intended to illuftrate. But the Minifter of the Marine would not give him the commiffion, fpite of the endeavours of Commander Bérard, Vice-Admiral under the Empire. The plates which Méryon completed, were badly received by the public, accuftomed as they were to fee his talents employed in the reprodu&tion of the pi&turefque fpots of Paris. Their execution, on which he brought to bear even more than his ordinary pains, upfet his brain and haftened his return to the hofpital at Charenton.

1ft St.   The edges of the work are unfinifhed.

2nd St.   With ' *Souvenir de Voyage*, MDCCCXLI–VI. *à Delâtre, imp. rue F. St. Jacques N. 81.*'   *h.* 8 in. *w.* 5¾ in.

61. *Le Malingue cryptogame.*

'One day' (fo wrote Méryon to Mr. Burty after having read the notice of his work in the *Gazette des Beaux-Arts*), 'in one of the walks which I ufed to take in order to pafs the time at the end of our fojourn at Akaroa, where we were placed to protect the French whalers, I faw in the corner of a wood of lofty foreft trees this poor little fungus. Its ephemeral exiftence probably only dated back to the morning which had followed a rainy night. Diftorted in form and pinched and puny from its birth, I could not but pity it. It feemed to me fo entirely typical of the inclemency, and at the fame time the whimficality, of an incomplete and fickly creation, that I could not deny it a corner in my "*fouvenirs de voyage*," and fo I drew it carefully, intending fome time or other to introduce it into one of my Akaroa fubjects.'

1ft St. In pure etching.

2nd St. With the monogram '*C. M.*' fometimes in red, fometimes in black.

3rd St. With the ferns for a background; the title, '*N. Z.* MDCCCXLV.' monogram in red, and beneath 'MDCCCXLV.' and '*P. Pierron imp.*'

This plate, etched on copper, only gave off a few impreffions.

h. 2⅞ in. *w.* 2¼ in.

62. Head of a New Holland Dog.

This little, but very expreſſive etching, was engraved on aluminium. It has been reproduced in facſimile in a book which abounds in reminiſcences of the country in which Méryon paſſed ſo happy a time. The work is entitled, *Quatre Années en Océanie. Hiſtoire naturelle de l'Homme et des Sociétés qu'il organiſe. Mœurs et coſtumes de certaines Papous Auſtraliens; Anatomie et phyſiologie du plus arrière des Noirs, par A. E. Foley. Paris: T. B. Baillière et Fils*, 1876.

Mr. A. E. Foley, retired Naval Lieutenant, but now a Doƈtor, in ſpeaking of the illuſtration at the end of the volume (vol. ii. p. 262), ſays :—' Tête d'un chien ſauvage de l'Auſtralie orientale, deſſinée d'après une eauforte qu'a faite mon défunt ami Charles Méryon, ancien officier de marine.'

1ſt St. The locks of hair are leſs marked, and the muzzle is leſs finely drawn than in the 2nd State.   *h.* 2¾ in. *w.* 2⅜ in.

63. Voyage de la Corvette 'Le Rhin'— Nouvelle Zélande. Greniers indigènes et habitations à Akaroa (Presqu'île de Banks), 1845.

The natives—men, women, and children—welcome a European. In the diſtance, to the right, ſtretch a foreſt and ſwelling hills.

1ſt St. In pure etching, before the ſky.
2nd St. With the ſky drawn in dry point.
3rd St. Before the monogram ' *C. M.*' and the title.
4th St. With the addreſs of the printer, A. Delâtre.

A proof was exhibited at the Salon in 1865. This and the following copper were etched in 1860.   *w.* 9½ in. *h.* 5½ in.

64. *Voyage de la Corvette 'Le Rhin'—Nouvelle Calédonie. Grand Cafe indigène fur le chemin de Ballorde à Poëpo, 1845.*

A woman carrying on her head a bafket of fruit, and a boy holding in his hands a large fifh, are directing their fteps towards a group of natives affembled before a hut.

1ft St.   In pure etching. The ground to the right of the plate nearly white.

2nd St.   Before the monogram '*C. M.*' in the fky or the marginal line at the top.

3rd St.   Before the addrefs of '*A. Delâtre, imp. rue Saint Jacques 245.*'

4th St.   With the title and addrefs.   *w.* 9⅜ in. *h.* 5⅜ in.

65. *Voyage du 'Rhin.' Océanie, Ilots à Uvea (Wallis). Pêche aux Palmes, 1845.*

Savages, immerfed in the water to their middle, are fifhing.

1ft St.   In pure etching, before the fky.

2nd St.   Before the marginal line completed and the crofs lines in the fky.

3rd St.   Finifhed, but before the title and before '*C. M. del. et fculp. 1863.*'

4th St.   With the addrefs of '*Pierron imp. r. Montfaucon 1.*'
                                            w. 13¼ in. *h.* 6¼ in.

G

66. *Nouvelle Zélande. Presqu'île de Banks, 1845. Pointe dite des Charbonniers à Akaroa. Pêche à la Seine.*

Fiſhing in a creek overhung by barren mountains.

1ſt St.   In pure etching.
2nd St.   With two boats alongſide the ſhore.
3rd St.   With one boat only, and with the addreſs of the printer Pierron (as in No. 65), and the title.   An impreſſion of this ſtate was exhibited in the Salon in 1864.   *w.* 12⅜ in. *h.* 6 in.

67. *Diverſes pièces gravées.   Collecte, gain, butin de courſe et de chaſſe, faits au mouillage et pendant le voyage à le Nouvelle Zélande, accompli de* MDCCCLII. *à* MDCCCXLVI. *par le Navire Rhin ſous les ordres de M. le Capitaine de Vaiſſeau (m·rt Contre-amiral en 1852), A. Bérard, Commandant la ſtation à Akaroa, preſqu'île de Banks, 1866.*

Trial proof.   In pure etching, ſimply in outline.
1ſt St.   The principal frame is ſtill empty.
2nd St.   With an indication in outline of the ſmaller frames, in which one reads in the following (3rd) ſtate to the left ' *Uvea, les Mulgraves, Tonga ;*' and to the right '*Ballade, Taïti, Onecke.*'
4th and laſt St.   With the addreſs '*Paris, C. M. Imp. rue Duperré 20,*' the whole forming the cover in which he ſold the ſmall etchings relative to his recollections of travel which follow.
w. 9½ in. *h.* 6 in.

68. *Nouvelle Zélande. Prefqu'île de Banks. Etat de la petite colonie françaife d'Akaroa vers 1845. Voyage du Rhin la chaumière du colon vieux foldat à Akaroa, Nᵉˑ Zélande, 1845.*

Trial proof in pure etching, before the clouds and the work on the mountains in the diftance.

1ft St. Before the lettering. A proof in Mr. Haden's collection has '7 Mai 66' in Méryon's writing.

2nd St. With the title and the publication line—'*C. M. del. Sculp. 1865,*' '*Pierron imp. rue Montfauçon,*' which will be found in the laft ftate of all this·feries. *h.* 3⅛ in. *w.* 3 in.

69. *Pré-volant des Iles Mulgraves Océanie.*

1ft St. Before the title at the top.

2nd St. With thefe words, '*La Harpe Oafienne.*' On an impreffion of this ftate in Mr. Burty's colleétion is written, in Méryon's handwriting, that he had only printed off 20 impreffions.

3rd St. With the letter '*I,*' or the No. '*1,*' on the waves.

4th St. With the word '*Rebus*' and the title.

h. 5¾ in. *w.* 3⅛ in.

70. *Petit Prince Dito* (*Ballade* N*elle.* Cal*e.*).

1ſt St.   With the word ' *Fantaſia.*'
2nd St.   With a ballad, which, however, has no rational interpretation, and with the publication line, ' *C. M. fct.* *Paris,* *Février, 1864, Pierron imp. Paris.*   Méryon repreſented the Prince as a ſavage, his head encloſed in a head-dreſs, or rather an enormous maſk, playing the flute and riding on a reſtive horſe.
h. 6¾ in. *w.* 5⅛ in.

71. *A Monſieur Eugène Bléry.*

.' *A vous, Bléry, mon maître,*
Qui m'avez fait connaître
Les ſecrets de votre art,

*   *   *   *

Ma muſe adoleſcente
De ſon unique avoir ·
Veut offrir le premice.'

It is not neceſſary to further tranſcribe the ſixteen verſes which compoſe this effuſion.

Mr. Eugène Bléry, who was born at Fontainebleau in 1805, has won ſeveral medals, and was decorated in 1846 for his painting and engraving.   He has been a continuous exhibitor of landſcapes, and ſtudies of trees and plants, drawn or etched after nature.   The foreſt of Fontainebleau, the neighbourhoods of Senliſſe and Cernay, having furniſhed him with the majority of his ſubjeéts.   He ſeems to have ſtudied the manner of J. T. Boiſſieu.

The plate has the publication line, ' *C. Méryon ft.* *Imp. rue* N*e.* S*t.* *Etienne du Mont, 26.*'   *h.* 5 in. *w.* 2¾ in.

72. *La Loi Lunaire.*

The Loi Lunaire was one of the firſt of the productions which ſhowed to Méryon's friends his mental derangement, more, perhaps, by the importance which he himſelf attached to it than by the ideas which it diſcloſed. He therein drew an upright box, or rather coffin, in which he propoſed that man and wife ſhould ſleep upright: his notion being that a horizontal poſition and the luxury of a bed weakened both mind and body. The general compoſition of the plate is, notwithſtanding, characteriſtic and powerful.

1ſt St.   Before the inſcription in the inner frame.

2nd St.   With the inſcription, the ſignature, and the publication line, '*C. M. imp. r. Dupêtre 20, Paris: D. 66.*'

h. 9⅚ in. w. 6¾ in.

73. *A ſecond plate of this Subject, on a ſmaller ſcale, and varying in many particulars.*

Only State.   In the left top corner the monogram, below to the left, '*C. M. imp. r. Dupêtre 20;*' to the right, '*Paris: Dʳ. 66.* h. 4⅛ in. w. 3¾ in.

74. *La Loi Solaire*.

The fun's rays fhine from behind, and at the lower angles of a tablet. Below an antique lamp is placed. On the tablet are the following fingular words in red and black :—

Si j'étais
Empereur ou Roi
De quelque puiffant état
(Ce que je ne voudrais ni ne pouvais être) ;—
Vu que les Grandes Cités ne fait enfantées
Que par la Pareffe, l'Avarice, la Crainte,
la Luxure, et autres mauvaifes paffions; je fe-
rais élaborée une loi, determinant d'une manière, auffi
précize que poffible, l'espace de terrain, avec ou
fans culture, forcement adjoint à toute habitation
de capacité voulue, pour un nombre donné de créatures
*humaines; de telle forte que l'*Air *et le* Soleil.
Ces deux principes effentiels de la Vie, *puis-*
fent toujours y être largement répartis.
Cette loi ; fource de tout bien matériel
et conféquemment moral, f'appellerait
Loi Solaire.

One ftate only, figned '*C. Méryon fit.*   *Paris,* MDCCCLV.
Imp: R. F. S. Jacques, 81.'   *h.* 4⅜ in. *w.* 3¼in.

75 & 76. *Trials for Engraving in Relief, by the aid of which Banknotes may be forged.*

On thefe trials, of which not more than two or three proofs at the outfide were taken, on a black ground are, the word '*France*,' a fragment of an Etrufcan frieze, a head of a woman, and growing plants.

1ft St.   Before a fort of reverfed *D*.

77 & 78. Rebuses.   Ci-gît la Vendetta Surannée, et Béranger ne fut véritablement fort, car il n'eut jamais la clef des chants.

77. On a block of ſtone is drawn a woman with a tub in front of her. She waſhes with a ſponge the letter '*D.*' The block reſts on the letters 'ANNÉE,' and above is another block, ſhaped like an anvil, on which is placed a ſledge-hammer. The whole is encloſed by a circle, round which is the date '*MDCCCLXIIII*,' and below in red the word '*Rebus.*' The publication line is '*C. M. fecit.   Pierron, imp., r. Montfaucon, 1.*

h. 3 in. w. 3 in.

78. A bird, ſome verſes, broken columns—a table with bottles and glaſſes and the inſcription '*Reſtaurateur en renom—Du Palais Royal*'—a fort ſeen from above with the inſcription '*Pays des Poulardes*'—a barrel labelled '*Pièce de Salaiſon*'—a bather— the croſs-bar of an anchor erect, ſurmounted by a wreath, and a key forming a monogram.

The titles, '*Chants myſtiques et maritimes—Chants nationaux —Chant religieux, chants guerriers, Marſeillaiſe—Chants populaires Elyſéens, Virgile, Homère.*

'*C. M. fecit 1863—chez Rochaux, Quai de l'Horloge 19; imp. Pierron, r. Montfaucon.*   h. 12 in. w. 5⅞ in.

There is but little to remark upon theſe rebuſes. They do not date from his laſt years, and conſequently they ſhow with what ſingular diſtractions he varied his more ſerious work.

There is a firſt ſtate of each befoie the publication line has been engraved with the burin.

79. *Defign for a frame for the Portrait of a Printer, epitomifing in an allegorical manner the hiftory of the invention and progrefs of Printing.*

The feries of ftates of this etching, which is of but little intereft from a purely artiftic point of view, is, in a manner, infinite. For a whole month Méryon, who lived near Mr. Burty, brought him nearly every morning a frefh proof. The frame was intended to contain the portrait of a printer and bookfeller at Fontenay, Vendée, M. Guéraud; it was ordered by an amateur, alfo a Vendean, and a well-known man of letters, M. Benjamin Fillon.

The following are the principal remarks on the ftates, of which we cannot give all, efpecially as the etching is never likely to be thought of much value:—

1ft St.   In pure etching.

2nd St.   Before the inner frame on the middle of the copper has been cut out.

3rd St.   Before the titles on the back of the volumes.

4th St.   With a *Lynx*, in the lower portion of the plate, upholding the book of the Code and the Laws.

5th St.   The Lynx has been effaced.

6th St.   The Lynx has been replaced by a fword placed before the book. Méryon's name to the right has been replaced by the name of the printer ' *A. Beillet.*'

7th St.   On the back of one of the books are feen the words ' *bains froids.*'

8th St.   Printed with a fecond plate in the centre, fhowing the portrait of M. Guéraud.   *h.* 6½ in. *w.* 5¾ in.

80. *Frontifpiece for a Catalogue of the Works of the Engraver,*
  Thomas de Léu.

M. Thomas Arnauldet, at that time attached to the Cabinet
des Eftampes, was about to publifh the catalogue of a draughtfman
and engraver, Thomas de Léu, a delicate and learned workman,
born at Paris about 1570, to whom we owe the portraits of
many of the celebrated perfonages of his time. He obtained
from Méryon this etching, the allegorical meaning of which is
very obfcure.

A man of emaciated appearance is feated at the foot of a tree;
he is fniffed at by a wolf, and a ferpent crawls at his feet. He
appears to be blinded by a ray which is reflected from a mirror
held by a woman who ftands in front of him. A fountain, in
the ftyle of the French Renaiffance, ferves as a bafe to a frame,
in which one reads the words, ' *Thomas de Léu. Effai du Catalogue*
de fon œuvre, précédé d'une notice hiftorique par Thomas Arnauldet.'
On fcrolls are the date ' *1579*,' and the names of the perfonages
whofe portraits Thomas de Léu has reproduced,—' *Bourbon,*
Lorraine, Montmorency,' alfo ' *1614* ' and ' *Briffon, Montaigne,*
Pafferet,' then ' *Portraits* ' and ' *P. de Brach, Lafphaife, Rouillard,*
Baugrand, Legagneur, W. Raleigh; ' on the fountain, ' *Paris,*
MDCCCLVI.' and on little frames the names of the artifts whofe
pictures Thomas de Léu reproduced,—' *Fournier, les Quefnel,*
Ant-Caron, T. Rabel, les Dumonftier, T. Bunel.'

1ft trial proof. Pure etching, in line.

2nd St. The folds of the draperies are more defined.

3rd St. Background is fhaded with horizontal lines.

4th St. The body of the man is modelled, except the arms:
a good deal of work is ftill wanting to complete the fountain.
All thefe trial proofs are before any lettering. This lettering,
as well as that of a large number of the etchings which he either
made or retouched after his return from the hofpital at Charenton,
were not written in by him, although he was an adept at handling
the burin, in little ftrokes. He told me that he had them done
by an artift who was efpecially good at this work, but he never
told me the name.

1ft St. Entirely finifhed. The entire plate has been worked
up by the burin. Méryon in the fecond period of his work,

that is, in all plates executed after the ' *Rue Pirouette aux Halles*,' deepened and widened the lines with an exceffively fharp burin; and as a confequence he hardly ever rebit his plates. I have, however, feen him feveral times rebite fmall parts of a copper, oftentimes five or fix confecutive times, with extreme patience, in order to obtain a richer tone than the brilliant but dry tone which is imparted by the burin.

2nd St. With ' *C. M. Del. et Sculp. 1866. Imp. Pierron rue Montfaucon 1, Paris.*

The copper-plate is in exiftence.   *h.* 6⅛ in. *w.* 4¼ in.

81. *Vue de l'ancien Louvre du Côté de la Seine en 1651.*

A large plate etched after a painting by Zeeman in the Louvre.

Trial proof in pure etching.

1ft St. Finifhed in a manner, and in this ftate delivered by Méryon to the Print-room of the Louvre.   Before any Letters.

2nd St. With the title.

The plate is in exiftence in the Print-room of the Louvre.

h. 10⅝ in. *w.* 6½ in.

82. *Le Miniſtère de la Marine.*

Trial proof, in pure etching, before the clouds.

1ſt St. With the drawings of boats, which float in the ſky, but before the ſabre thrown to the ground in the ſtreet.

2nd St. With the figures and boats in the ſky, the ſword on the ground, and the monogram ' *C. M.*' in the centre of the lower margin.

3rd St. With the title and the addreſs of '*A. Cadart, imprimeur éditeur.*'

The plate was publiſhed by the French Etching Club, and is in exiſtence.   *h.* 6⅓ in. *w.* 5¾ in.

83. *Collège Henri IV.*

This large plate was a commiſſion from Méryon's two old friends, Meſſieurs Philipon and Salicis, and is ſtill their property. A conſiderable portion of it is fantaſtically conceived, and is eaſily diſtinguiſhed from the remainder, which is moſt faithfully exaćt. Mr. Burty once had in his poſſeſſion ſketches of ſeveral portions of the ſubjećt, which had been drawn in ſmall fragments, and then pieced together.

Méryon wrote a long deſcriptive letter anent his extraordinary produćtion. It appeared in 1864 in the journal *L'Union des Arts.* The following are charaćteriſtic extraćts from it, and relate to the firſt ſtate of the plate :—

'*Toute la partie gauche de ma gravure eſt occupée par une ſuite de perſonnages gliſſant ou patinant. Qu'il me ſoit permis de dire que maintenant que j'ai fait une aſſez dure expérience de la vie, je conſidère cette pratique comme fort importante pour les jeunes gens.* . . . *Le trois petits perſonnages le plus à gauche cauſent ou diſcutent* . . . *Suivant l'importance de la penſée que j'y ai attaché, la figure qui repréſente la Généroſité eſt beaucoup plus grande que les autres. J'ai pris en outre cette licence de ſuppoſer de la glace, ſuivant une partie de le façade du premier plan, quoique près de-là les arbres foient garnis des leurs feuilles.'*

In a firſt ſtate, which he called ' *réſervé, et tiré à 40 épreuves,*' Méryon had connedted fantaſy with reality, by placing in the ſky, contiguous to the college buildings, certain remembrances of his travels, of which this was his explanation :—

'*Cette ſorte de triangle ou fedteur placé au-deſſus des deux divinités marines, d'où ſ'épand la lumière ſur toute la compoſition fantaſtique, peut rappeler le triangle myſtique et même cet inſtrumcnt, muni de ce qu'on appelle* grand *et* petit *miroir, à l'aide deſquels les navigateurs déterminent leur poſition ſur le globe. Cette boule noire qui ſe voit ſur le devant de la voile de la première embarcation, eſt la coïffure, en formз de bonnet de grenadier, d'un maſque particulier en uſage dans une danſe de la Nouvelle-Calédonie. Sur cette même voile ſe détache un oiſeau, les ailes à moitié fermées, qui fond ſur quelque proie, à la manière de l'oiſeau de mer connu ſous le nom commun de* fou. *A l'aplomb de cet oiſeau, ſur le plate forme de la pirogue, poſé obliquement ſur un foyer d'où l'échappe de la fumée, le pot ou marmite ſphérique où ces naturels font cuire le produit de leur pêche. Dans le coin de gauche, monts, habitans, champs cultivés, petits perſonnages dont on diſtingue pluſieurs ſur le ſommet du pic, viaduc lointain avec train, font alluſion aux péripeties des voyages. . . .*'

In an early impreſſion in the colledtion of Mr. Haden the ' *Boule noire*' has not yet been inſerted, nor in the left upper corner are there any of the ' *monts, champs cultivés,*' &c. The plate is bare of anything to the left of the large tower and the line of buildings beneath it ; the ſky, too, is unfiniſhed, and has not yet received its ' *ſorte de triangle.*'

2nd St. Méryon, after having completed the left portion of the ſky, inſcribed on the right lower margin of the plate a long, explanatory notice, which it is hardly neceſſary to ſet out here.

3rd St., of which ten impreſſions were taken off. On the ſea is to be ſeen a ſmall ſteamboat, and in the centre the monogram, '*C. M.*'

About ſeventy impreſſions in all of the foregoing ſtates having been taken off, Méryon eraſed the unnatural part of the work, and finiſhed his plate from nature, but it muſt needs be ſaid with the reſult of making it very heavy. This is what he wrote as to the change :—

'*Dans cette pièce, reproduдtion textuelle et minutieuſe de la réalité, j'ai appoſé au milieu du trait ſupérieur deux médaillons portant les effigies des deux souverains sous l'invocation desquels est placé le Lycée (Henri IV. et Napoléon III. en statues équestres). Entre ces médaillons, une tablette sur laquelle on lit la devise latine par laquelle je me suis proposé de résumer le pensée qui avait présidé à mon œuvre.*

'*Dans cet état, le fond est en tous points gravé avec une précision allant presque jusqu'à la minutie. Je citerai, vers le centre du college, à la façade du corps de logis mitoyen donnant sur une des cours, un cadran solaire en pierre, l'élevant sur le toit ; dans le coin à gauche, une partie de Saint-Etienne du Mont et de l'Ecole polytechnique ; dans l'angle en haut et à droite, Saint-Médard ; tout-à-fait à la limite du coin de gauche, le pavillon d'entrée, sur le quai, de l'entrepôt des vins ; au-dessous du médaillon de droite, la prison de Sainte-Pélagie, où l'on peut distinguer les guérites des factionaires, et sur les crêtes des toits, les petites voies de pierre qui les relient. A l'aplomb encore de ce médaillon, vers le centre, en partie dans l'ombre, l'entrée de la rue Copeau, où l'on aperçoit sur le pavé quelques passants.*

'*Usant de mon droit d'auteur pour cette pièce, j'ai indiqué par mes initiales C. et M. (avec une petite croix entre les deux lettres) une maison, Rue Saint-Etienne du Mont, 26, que j'ai habitée pendant un assez long laps de temps, où j'ai fait ma suite intitulée '* Eaux-fortes *sur Paris.' A proximité, une autre où j'ai connu un peu, ou plutôt vu et entendu quelquefois une jeune fille dont je m'étais inconsidérément épris à cause surtout de sa fort gracieuse voix, laquelle me mit plus d'une fois à la torture, et qui eut une assez grande influence sur certains évènements de ma vie, mais influence plutôt, hélas ! néfaste.'*

This state bore the inscription, '*Vu: à vol d'oiseau du Collége Henri IV. ou Lycée Napoléon.'*

4th St. A fresh description, shorter but not much clearer, was engraved in the centre of the lower margin, and in this condition, with the address of the printer, the plate was published.

w. 19 in. *h.* 11¾ in.

84. *Bain froid, Chevrier, dit de l'Ecole.*

One of the bathing-fheds on the Seine.

Trial proof, in pure etching, before the fky and the fhadows on the baths. In Mr. Haden's collection.

1ft St. Copper, 6¾ in. *w.* 5⅛ *h.*, before the monogram, '*C. M.*'

2nd St. Copper, cut to 5⅝ in. *w.* 5⅛ in. *h.* with '*Bain froid, Chevrier,*' on a board above the baths.

3rd St. The title, publication line, and monogram. Ten impreffions were ftruck off with a verfe, etched on another copper, printed thereon in blue ink.

Mr. Haden has the drawings for this etching, figned '*C. M. 1864.*'

Division No. IV.
Portraits.

---

85. 'Portrait of Meryon, three-quarter length, seated before an Easel.'

No impreſſions of this were kept by Méryon. It was he who informed me of its exiſtence. It was one of his firſt attempts at *engraving*, and was originally oval in form.

86. 'Portrait of Mons. Decourtive, Scholar of Medicine, Author of "A Thesis on the Hadswick."'

This portrait was etched by Méryon whilſt under the influence of Rembrandt. We only know of one proof, and that is cut down.

Méryon has repreſented his friend three-quarter length, ſeated, and having near him a violin and chemical utenſils. He has a high forehead, flowing locks thrown back, and a penetrating look. The light illumines brightly the left of his face.

The diſtance from the chin to the top of the hair is about 2 inches.

87. 'PORTRAIT OF M. EUGÈNE BLÉRY, AFTER BUTTERA.'

We are unable to give any particulars of this portrait, having never feen a copy, and only being cognifant that it exifts.

88. 'PORTRAIT OF MONS. CASIMIR LECOMTE.'

The initials '*G. B.*' are thofe of the painter, '*Gustave Boulanger.*' This was a facfimile of his drawing.

The portrait of Monf. Cafimir Lecomte is three-quarter length. He is reprefented as feated, the head bare, one of his hands is paffed beneath his waiftcoat, the other holds his cane and his hat.

1ft St. In pure etching, before '*C. Méryon del aqua-forte, 1856, d' après G. B.*'

2nd St. With the infcription.   *h.* 13⅜ in. *w.* 10⅜ in.

89. *Evarifte Boulay-Paty.*

This portrait, treated with great care, was etched after a medallion in bronze of the fculptor David of Angers. It was intended to be placed at the commencement of a collection of poetry.

1ft St. Before any lettering.

2nd St. Before '*C. M. fc. 1861,*' but with the addrefs, '*Delâtre Imp. r. des Feuillantines à Paris.*'

3rd St. With both monogram and addrefs.

                    Diameter, 4¼ in.

90. *François Viète.*

A portrait copied from a frontifpiece of a work written by this celebrated mathematician. It appeared in Nos. 92, 93, and 95, in the fecond volume of a work publifhed by Monf. Benjamin Fillon, with the title, '*Poitou et Vendée.*' It is almoft entirely re-engraved with the burin. It gave a great amount of trouble to Méryon, who was at the time very ill. There are many different trial proofs, and we have only here mentioned the principal.

Trial proof, in pure etching. Before the cloak.

1ft St. With the cloak, fhaded, and with fantaftic figures.

2nd St. With the monogram '*C. M.*,' a roll of manufcript, cheffmen, &c., and '*A. Beillet imp.*'

3rd St. Finifhed, with the lettering as above. It alfo bears the addrefs, '*A. Beillet, quai de la Tournelle 35, a Paris.*'

h. 7⅜ in. *w.* 4¼ in.

91. *Pierre Nivelle, évêque de Lucon, né à Troyes en 1584, mort à Lucon le 10 Fév. 1660.*

An oval portrait in an allegorical framework. After an old engraving. Etched on tin.

Trial proof, in pure etching.

1ft St. Finifhed, with '*D'après M. L. Imp. A. Beillet, Q. de la Tournelle 35, Paris.*' *h.* 6⅝ in. *w.* 4¼ in.

H

92. *T. Agrippa d'Aubigné.*

A copy, or perhaps rather a free-hand interpretation, of a lithograph portrait, figned Hibert, of this celebrated leader of the Calvinifts. The lithograph being after the picture preferved by the Council at Geneva.

1ft St.   Before any lettering.
2nd St.   With the title, ' *C. M. d'après H^t. Imp. A. Beillet, Q. de la Tournelle 35, Paris.*'
3rd St.   Entirely reworked. The tin—for it was on this material that the picture was engraved—is cut clofe up to the marginal lines.   *h.* 4⅞ in. *w.* 4 in.

93. *Jean Befley, d'après L. Ifac, æt. 70, ann. 1642.*

Jean Befley was one of the hiftorians of the province of Poitou.

1ft St.   Before the margins of the plate were cleaned, before the marginal line, and before a great deal of fubfequent work.
2nd St.   Before the monogram ' *C. M.*'
3rd St.   With the monogram and title, ' *Jean Befley, 1861, d'après L. Ifac. Imp. A. Beillet, Q. de la Tournelle 35.*'
h. 5⅝ in. *w.* 4½ in.

94. *René de Burdigale, Sr. de Laudonnière, Sablais, d'après Crifpin de Pas.*

An oval portrait, in an emblematical frame, after an old engraving.

1ſt St.   In pure etching.
2nd St.   Before the initials ' *C. M.*'
3rd St.   With the device, ' *Si Dieu me garde, j'iray à fin,*' and the publication line, ' *A. Beillet, Imp. Quai de la Tournelle 35, Paris.*'   *h.* 6 in. *w.* 4⅛ in.

95. ' PORTRAIT OF THE PRINTER, ARMAND GUÉRAUD, FROM A PHOTOGRAPH.'   ·

This little, ſquare, and truly hideous portrait, was placed in the emblematical frame juſt deſcribed. It was engraved with the burin on a ſoft metal—tin—which only gave off a few proofs.

96. *Louis Jacques Marie Bizeul.*

Portrait of a Breton archæologift, from a photograph.

Trial proof. Pure etching.

1ft St. With fome burin work, with the burr unremoved on the overcoat.

2nd St. With certain lines of the burin extending over the edges and not effaced.

3rd St. Finifhed, but before the title.

4th St. With the title and '*C. M. fculpt. 1861, imp. Beillet, Paris,*' and above '*75me. année de fon âge.*'   *h.* 6½ in. *w.* 4⅝ in.

97. *Benjamin Fillon.*

· This portrait, which was taken from a photograph, exaggerates—nay, almoft caricatures—the energetic, but never *ferocious*, countenance of M. Benjamin Fillon.

Trial proof, in pure etching.

1ft St. Before the title.

2nd St. With the title.

Alphabetical Index of Etchings.

Numerical Index of Etchings.

LONDON :

Printed by STRANGEWAYS & SONS, Tower Street, St. Martin's Lane.

www.ingramcontent.com/pod-product-compliance
Lightning Source LLC
Chambersburg PA
CBHW032102010726
47493CB00008B/2505